SPLASH OF INK

SPLASH OF INK

Edited by A M Howcroft

InkTears
The Granary,
Purston,
Brackley,
Northants,
NN13 5PL

ISBN 978-1-910207-38-3

Dedicated to

the readers and writers of InkTears

Contents

INTRODUCTION

by A M Howcroft

I might as well start by admitting that I wasn't a big fan of flash fiction, when I first started the short story publisher InkTears in 2009. The examples I had come across seemed too fragmentary, too short for me to care about the characters, and didn't conjure any strong emotions or reactions. Yes, there was Hemmingway's famous six-word story, but that's not what I call literature. Thanks (possibly) to the Internet, flash fiction was having something of a revival, with more work being published, and new contests emerging. I was entering my own short stories into competitions, and occasionally appearing at literary events to read or if I was very lucky, to collect a prize. It seemed that everywhere I went, David Gaffney was reading his flash fiction pieces – and these, I loved. They were funny, full of empathy and understanding of people and their quirks. For the first time I began to see that flash could be different. As an experiment, I decided to try running a flash fiction contest at InkTears. It would completely change the way I looked at short fiction.

Our main InkTears short story contest has always been a big affair, with ten judges, several rounds of reading and selecting, which takes a fair amount of organization, time and effort from many people. Before the days of the wonderful online service *Submittable*, all short story contests had to work out how to manage entries themselves, and there used to be one day a year where I printed out the opening page of each story in our contest, and sorted them into alphabetical order for the 'snap-judge' round. Opening several hundred documents and printing just the first page is a tiresome task and sorting them was even worse. My one-day effort frequently stretched over an entire week, and since this was always in December – not the quietest time of the year – it was something of a headache. I was determined that the flash contest would be simpler. I was also not sure how many entrants we would have in our first contest, or if it would become a regular event. What's more, I didn't know if I could rely on my regular judges to pitch-in for the flash contest. I was already asking them to do a pile of work each Christmas and New Year, unpaid. Therefore, I decided to judge the contest myself.

I can't remember the exact number of entries that first year. It was in the hundreds. The contest was timed to run early in the season, so that I could read and review the pieces while the short story contest was open, and then we could announce the results before the short story judging began in December. Somehow, I found myself with a looming deadline, and a schedule that required me to read twenty or so entries a day. At 500 words each, that's 10,000 words – equivalent to a sizeable chunk of a novel, every evening. I did the judging online, which saved a lot of paper and time, but it was still tough to get through all the entries and inform the winners on time. Exhausted, I vowed to do things differently next time. Yet in late October of the next year, I was again reading upwards of thirty flash pieces a night. I vowed, for the second time, to change. In the contest's third year, when I saw the growth in the number of entries, and did some mental calculations, I realised I really had to change. I began reading a handful of stories every day, from the moment the contest closed. What I discovered, was that I rapidly came to really enjoy my reading time, when the pressure was not on. The standard of the entries varied, but there was always something of interest in the items I read. I had become a flash fan.

What really changed my perception, though, was when I first started to find little vignettes that wouldn't leave my head. Compelling pieces, as powerful as any short story, these were small, benevolent viruses that infected my mind, and made me want to tell everyone about them. Flash stories like *August-the-Fourth-1979* by Sal Page, which to this day I find totally compelling. Or *Lost and found* by Emma Viskic, which moves me to tears almost every time I read it. In many ways, I find them like poetry, or a song, able to trigger an emotional response and stay with you for a long period. Over the years of reading several thousand entries in our contests, I have come to see flash fiction as a genuinely unique art form, something with its own niche that slides between short stories, poetry, and music.

I always read the stories blind, which is to say I don't check who wrote the piece until the final round of judging. Despite this, I began to see the same names appearing frequently in our winners and shortlists. Ingrid Jendrzejewski and Amanda Huggins share the record for success, with four published pieces each in this volume. I love the way Ingrid captures slices of life that are meaningful and thoughtful, often with fabulous direct dialogue such as in *Sign, signifier, signified*, or the reported conversation in *Moby Dick and the beginning of the end.*

2

While Amanda has displayed a broad range of writing styles and subjects, often touching on themes such as grief and tragedy in the seemingly effortless but powerful *Scratched enamel heart*, and *Your own child*. It was no surprise to see Amanda publish her own collection of stories, and I see Ingrid going from strength to strength, appearing at festivals and collecting prizes wherever she goes.

There are several other writers that appear more than once in this collection; Jude Higgins, Kerry Hood, Amanda O'Callaghan and Sharon Telfer. These are names that can be found frequently in the pages of other magazines and anthologies. There were also several writers that have had success in both our flash and short story contests, and span both genres with equal comfort. Right from the start, though, I've been delighted to see how many new writers we have been able to publish, both young and old. When I reached out to the writers included in this volume, to let them know the details of the anthology, half a dozen told me that InkTears was the first site to ever publish a piece of their work. That gives me a warm glow inside, and is rather humbling, too. I like to think that flash is less intimidating to a new writer, it feels like something anybody can do. That doesn't mean it's easy and as the adage goes - there are less words in a poem than a novel, but each word is chosen with extreme care. There is some of that truth in flash, too. By encouraging new writers, we get to see unique perspectives. I love *The unexpected arrival of the black guy* by Charlotte Josephs for this reason, along with *Messenger* by Brian Wilson.

The subjects and themes have been incredibly varied; we have horror, sci-fi, romance, and some of my favourite stories have had a touch of the surreal: *A nightcap with Bukowski* by Morgan Roberts, for example. Then there are several prose poems; *Pocket wishes for scraps of paper* by John Heggelund or *Things that used to be safe* by Natalia Theodoridou. We have even published one story that has never been claimed, where the writer disappeared and despite numerous efforts, we were never able to trace her. I often think there are many stories hidden within the stories.

I wish I could highlight each flash piece in this introduction, give each author another moment of recognition, but that is what InkTears has already done via our website and newsletter. Now, I must leave the discovery to you, the readers. I have no doubt you will find your own favourites within these pages. I can tell you that every one of these tiny gems has moved me enough to award it a prize in our

3

annual contest. Reading through them again, I'm delighted by the quality of work we have had the honour of publishing, and hope that by putting this collection together we can bring the joy of flash to more people.

Here's a final little secret that I'll leave you with. I have one simple reason why I've published this book. I want a copy on my bookshelf. Long after digital formats have morphed into some new variant and our InkTears website has been left in the dust, I want to be able to pull this book off the shelf and re-read these pieces. I want to pass the book on to my daughter so she can do the same. I hope you care as passionately about the writing as I do. Enjoy.

Church

by Scott Whittaker

The church at the end of my street has its own TV show. Not TV like primetime, but TV like channel 978. And it's not, strictly speaking, the church's show. The church is always in the show, but that doesn't make it the church's show, apparently. The pastor says it's the congregation's show. But it seems to me that the congregation, like the church, is just in the show. The pastor told me I have a strange way of thinking about things. Which struck me as a strange comment, coming from the pastor of a church with its own TV show.

The pastor's forehead furrows extend right over the curve at the top of his skull. His dog collar hangs out stiff and sideways. And he lives with a monkey. It sits at his table and presses its face against the windows, both hands flat on the glass. Maybe it's the monkey's TV show, really. The monkey is there to show how the Bible is right. The pastor takes it to places and insists it's his relative. They film it.

The first one, they took the monkey to a restaurant and filmed it smashing up the table and screeching. When the manager asked them to leave, they filmed him and the pastor while the pastor insisted that the monkey was his relative and should be treated kindly. The manager declined the invitation and offered to call the police. They show that on the show and the pastor he says after it that, that proves it: no way we're related to monkeys - they can't even eat a lasagne with a fork.

It must have gone over well. The pastor rang up airlines and told them he needed a seat for his relative and they said OK. Then he told them it was a monkey and they said he'd have to go in the hold; they couldn't have a monkey running around the cabin. And the pastor came on the screen and said, that proves it, see? Darwin was an idiot.

Pastor took the monkey to all the local businesses. He wanted his monkey to take tennis lessons, get a haircut, join a gym. They all said no. The monkey looked disappointed.

The pastor said to me, he thought it was the best way to prove to people that no-one really believed in the theory of evolution. I said I believed in it.

The next morning, he's at my place with the cameras. Wants to rent a van. I said, *Does your relative have a credit card?* Turned out he didn't, so the pastor had to use his. *That's fine,* I said. *Does your relative have a driving license?* I said, *No worries, we'll just put it under your name.* Pastor looked a little more furrowed, but he signed the paperwork and I got him his van. The monkey looked pleased, climbing up into the cab.

C'mon Pastor, I said. *Start it up for him.*

The days to come

by Michael Batchelor

I don't think you mind our silence; we've fallen into it quite naturally. You're watching the bar, which doubles as a reception for an upstairs hostel, and I'm watching you, your face in profile.

Together, we're alone, sat by the far wall, and set apart from others by our silence, our sobriety. We're making the room louder; I wonder if you've noticed. I wonder what you're thinking.

I follow your eyes. You're watching a crowd of people vie for the attention of the bar staff. Among them, other backpackers wade about with confused looks on their red, wind-weathered faces. I watch as someone hoists a bag onto one shoulder. A drink is spilt, a glass smashed. The crowd ripples and breaks. Now you're staring at the floor.

I could read you better when you were speaking; you seemed to lose your composure. You shifted your weight, and you snatched at things with your fingers. You spoke nervously, despite, I'm sure, having practiced your lines.

I asked about home, about your work-life, and you faltered. You appeared unwilling to tell me the truth, but apparently you hadn't yet prepared anything else. I found this strange, as you must have been asked these questions before. I'm now wondering, though: was it that you were *tempted* to tell me the truth? Was it that you were tired of lying?

I remember, you took a breath, and angled your face away from mine. "I don't know," you said, as is your habit. "I don't know." And with that, we aborted the conversation.

Now, you look weary, leaning back in your chair. You're clearly preoccupied. You're languishing under the weight of what you're not telling me.

And what *are* you telling me, exactly? I've learnt your name, of course, and your nationality. I've heard about your travels; I've listened to your tales. But, still, I know nothing about your life. I don't know why you're here.

I know that tomorrow you'll be flying home. You'll be returning to something that, one month ago, you felt the need to leave. I wonder if you're ready. I wonder what you're thinking.

In your eyes, I see defeat, I see surrender. You'll go quietly, I think. As though led by captors, agents of fate. Back to a pain that's been temporarily forgotten. To thoughts and feelings that you might have hoped to escape.

In the airport, you'll have come full circle. You'll have returned to your starting point, and you'll be struck by everything you were feeling when you were last there, stood by the bagel stand, or the toilets. You'll feel as though you're watching your old self, and you'll regret not having done more. You'll regret that nothing's changed.

I'm speculating, of course. But I can see that you're unhappy, and that, already, something's obsessing you. Your head's turned, and you're staring into the middle distance. You're waiting for the night to pass. You're probably thinking about the days to come.

Their memories

by Jude Higgins

I said everyone has a memory of walking through a field of corn, and you said it wasn't corn, it was rye and you watched me pulling off a handful of grains to eat like I'd done ever since I was a child and waited until I was about to put them in my mouth before you said that rye gets a fungus called ergot and ergotism can cause both physical and mental harm, including convulsions, miscarriage, necrosis of digits, hallucinations and death. And I said, why did you have to wait until I was about to eat them before you told me and what is necrosis anyway?

So after that I stopped speaking to you for a while and made a point of eating all the unwashed strawberries from the carton we'd bought in the lay-by from the people in the clapped-out van, as if I couldn't care less that the berries had probably been sprayed with goodness-knows-what. You walked on in front of me, snapping off the long stalks and when we reached the common where the path was overgrown with bracken, you said I should have worn trousers, ticks love bracken. You said you'd got some waterproofs in your rucksack, I could put on – I didn't want to get Lyme's Disease, did I? And I said if I'd already contracted ergotism what would it matter? You said I hadn't eaten any rye, had I, you'd stopped me – and not to be so childish, you were only trying to look after me, like you always did. And I said I don't want to be looked after, I'm a grown woman. And you said, well act like one then.

I reminded you this was the second row we'd had a field of grain. The first was when we were on that long walk and you said you could find the way home by looking at the way lichen grew on trees but when night fell we were lost and you led us on a so-called short cut through a field littered with great spools of hay. The night was humid, we'd been walking for hours and I said we had to have a rest and that you were an idiot. You said you weren't an idiot; everyone should get lost once in a while, that's what made life exciting and I said it didn't have to be on a day when it looked like thunder. It won't thunder you said so I spread out our picnic blanket next to one of the spools and we shared a Snickers bar you found in your pocket and watched the moon come out. I remember that Snickers bar, you said, it tasted really good. It did, I said – do you remember the moon? And you smiled and said yes, it was a good memory. Then you rummaged in your rucksack, brought out a Mars bar and gave me the first bite.

Teeth

by Maureen Gallagher

This house has grown teeth. They certainly weren't here when I moved in last year. I know that for a fact because I paid an engineer good money to give it the once-over. And that man was thorough. The sort that wouldn't blink an eye at slithering down a drain or shooting up a loft, iPod in one hand, lump hammer in the other. At the time, he pointed out a missing tile or two, a few plaster cracks, the need for a lick of paint. But teeth? Definitely no mention of teeth. He zipped around the house like a forensic scientist, banging on walls, pipes, fittings. Not a crooked thumbtack holding up a gas arrears bill on the underside of the antique pine corner-unit escaped his beady eye. Definitely no pearlies.

They're here now. I hear them at night. Grinding. Sabres sharpening up for a showdown. I lie in bed imagining canines lengthening by the minute and I drift off to a jungle – alligators everywhere snapping off legs, arms, even heads; travel farther south to where starving dingos, capable of finishing off a writer at one sitting, lie in wait.

You don't expect your house to have teeth, like some evolutionary aberrant, some mutant with the slimmest chance of driving progress. I'm sick of it. I called my dentist out for a home visit. It cost a fortune and he refused to do a goddamn thing. Said I should go visit a head doctor. But what would a head doctor know about teeth?

August-the-fourth-1979

by Sal Page

Alice had just filled the car up with petrol and was heading to the shop to pay when August-the-fourth-1979 surfaced from some half-forgotten area of her brain, what she imagined was the swampy part behind the back of her neck, a place for dark and dreadful thoughts to lurk. She could go for months without thinking about August-the-fourth-1979 then, for no discernible reason, it would rear its head for a holiday in the conscious part of her brain.

As she slipped into the shop and joined the queue, Alice tried humming it away with snatches of speeded up 'Dancing Queen' but that didn't work. She felt hot and fanned her face ineffectually with a flapping hand. She reminded herself that Paddy had been dead years and even if he was still alive he probably wouldn't remember what she had said that day. Some people were lucky. They never remembered anything. Or so it seemed to Alice.

The words she'd uttered all those years ago skipped and skittered around her brain, teasing her and making her stomach lurch. She cringed and tried replacing her idiotic words with a plan for grilled salmon later and another attempt at hollandaise sauce. Was there an egg left? Alice couldn't think. Sights, sounds and feelings that accompanied her words were starting to crowd their way in. It was like she was back in August-the-fourth-1979 all over again.

There were only two people in front of her. She changed the salmon to a meat and potato pie and thought about gravy and flaky pastry but August-the-fourth-1979 was still making its presence felt. She reached the till and, getting flustered, put her PIN in wrong. Twice.

The woman glared at her. "You have one more chance."

All of her

by Louise Kennedy

Why, of course I remember the first day I brought Andrew here. I was still a teenager, showing off my artist beau. Christina had been in the garden and was making her way to the house. She was reaching and dragging across the ground in that way she had of getting around without a wheelchair; so strange yet so natural to her. I remember how Andrew stared down at her, and how I wished he hadn't. People looked at Christina slyly but they normally didn't stare.

I don't recall if she was wearing the pink dress that day. A quart or more of blueberries was cupped in a sling around her neck, her arms and face mottled purplish black, like fresh bruising.

Whenever she was asked, she said that she liked 'Christina's World'. She said she liked the neat, pale swathe of grass in front of the house, and the way Andrew had moved the barn away slightly, widened the view.

"Or that's what he told me he did, although I didn't know really what he meant, just that "it worked"," she said.

She said she liked how you can see every blade of grass, because that is what she could see.

"He said he had painted the house and grass first then added me in the foreground and that the pink jumped out for him. Foreground. I ask you.   As far as I'm concerned there's just the ground," she said.

I think her arms shocked her, how thin they had become. At least Andrew had made them look smooth, not stringy and knotted at the elbow, the way they really were. She thought they looked strange in the painting, though, like a hook that's missing an eye, she said.

Did she like it? I wonder. It's because of the Helga paintings, you see; all those nudes that Andrew painted in secret. I think of Christina often now. I think of her when I imagine Andrew tracing Helga's breasts and thighs with slow strokes of his brush, in private, away from me. I think of Christina on days when I can think of almost nothing else. I look at 'Christina's World' now and see what Christina must have seen. The cocked hips are fecund, full of promise, the stray strand of hair wanton. They were mine. The spindly limbs were hers, and the dress. The womanly parts he took from me. He painted every blade of grass, but didn't paint all of her.

Clockwork

by Russell Reader

"What time am I being picked up?" she asks for the fifth time in as many minutes.

"You're not being picked up today, I've come to see you – I always come to see you on Wednesdays, remember? Two until three?"

"Oh yes, come to see me", she repeats, looking restful for a minute or so, smiling. It doesn't last long. "What time am I being picked up?"

She'd shown a sudden spark on my last visit, launching into a conversation about last night's Emmerdale. For a moment I thought she was back. But then she stopped mid-sentence and her face went blank again, like somebody had just done a force quit on her memory bank. Gone.

I always feel guilty when I glance at my watch, but I can't help it; it's painful sitting here, repeating the same thing over and over, seeing her like this, wiry hair everywhere, roots showing, a blouse that doesn't match her skirt. She used to be such an elegant woman. Twinset and pearls, that type.

I rummage in my pockets for my car keys. Left one. Right one. Must be in my bag.

"They're on the side", she says, quick as a flash. "You put them there every week, next to the clock."

110th and 3rd

by Tamzin Merchant

The man in the stolen overcoat offered death with his left hand. I could tell it was stolen because it had the price tag still on it and a plastic security sensor stapled to the arm. Somewhere, I imagined, an alarm had screamed briefly as he'd bolted from the shop.

He said, "You're getting to be an endangered species round here."

Perhaps he'd snuck into cheesy B-movies to get out of this New York cold: stolen in, in his stolen overcoat, and now he was stealing lines from stolen stories.

I couldn't look the gun in the eye. I kept it in the edges of my vision like a snake that might spit. Around us the winter lights of Third Avenue seemed to wheel like a carousel, all gold and playful and making me feel sick.

I said, "I guess you want my purse."

He held out a hand - his right - for it. It shook as if all the traffic coming down through the arteries of the Park was oscillating up through his feet on the concrete sidewalk and agitating his body.

I was shaking just as much.

He said, "You cold?"

I said, "Yes."

I said, "You?"

He said, "Yes."

The gun said nothing.

I slid the purse down into the crook of my elbow and onto my wrist. My coat made my movements blunt. I held it out on my hand with the purse straps hanging over it, red against white. I'd forgotten my gloves.

He took the bag, weighed it thoughtfully and stuck the gun in his coat pocket.

It was my time to run away. Instead, I watched as he peered into my purse, and felt he was peering into my opened chest through my skin, careful as a heart-surgeon. He reached a hand inside and pulled out my wallet. He handed me back the purse and I took it.

"Thank you," I said.

He opened the wallet and took out a $20.

"That's all I had in there," I said.

As snow came down from the dark yellow sky he smiled.

He folded the bill and tucked it into the inner breast pocket of that big square-shouldered overcoat, closed the wallet neatly and handed it back.

"Thank you", I said again, "Do you have a cigarette?"

He put his hand back in his pocket and pulled out a crumpled packet, tapped one out and lit it in his mouth. He handed it to me between his fingers and dragging on it felt like a kiss.

The way he turned made it feel like a song. He walked away down the snowy avenue.

The swing doors were glass and bronze, burnished with light from inside. My fingers were stinging with sudden warmth and nicotine.

I sat down on the floor of the elevator as it carried me upward.

Olympic café

by Kerry Hood

The second word fell off so long ago that it doesn't look missing. What is left in blue plastic letters is O L Y M P I C, wonky but hanging on. In the flat above, behind yellow drapes, is Nikos, by the bed that landed him fifty years ago, watching his father George's heavy-hearted sleep. His mother watches too, trapped in a frame, alive only in aromas from downstairs (the oldest Greek place this side of London). Sometimes, when Nikos is working in the kitchen, he'll imagine he sees her through the steam, sending out dishes of spinach pie and stuffed marrow. He'll inhale a feather of rosemary to bring her palm to his cheek.

Downstairs right now, Nikos's sister places thick coffee and honey biscuits on white tables, pushed together tonight for the others on this street also bullied: the Five Rings jeweller; the manager of Bar Twenty Twelve; the owner of Gold Medal Sports; the vicar who advertised a 'Summer 2012' fete; and a few more who come to ask who owns the words? To bang fists beneath the tapestry of Mount Olympus with the same rage that made Nikos's grandfather hunt fascists in black caves. The same rage that burns Athens. The same protest that flattens his father here.

Nikos feels the old man's forehead, the deep tracks of a once faster, higher, stronger being who has lived to serve plates of sunshine but who now unwittingly offends sponsors of junk food. The café George has owned for a half-century so enrages these invisible giants that they send letters via thick-necked couriers demanding he changes what is left of the name in order to Uphold The Spirit Of The Games.

So this afternoon he lay down. He recited to the ceiling stories of ancient contests fought for honour by free Greeks – heroes, warriors, thinkers. 'But today', George said, 'we are slaves.' He made Nikos rearrange the blue plastic letters to read

I C O M P L Y

and now father and son drowse, wonky, hanging on, unaware

that someone is photographing this new sign and sending it on an electronic baton around the world.

It is George who wakes in the early light to ask about the noise. It is Nikos who squints around the sun-stain drapes. It is a sea of humans that blinks back. Rippling beyond the cramped street, heads upturned, standing elbow to elbow or on car roofs or the shoulders of others: the poets and sculptors and wrestlers and runners and Big Issue sellers and smallholders and stallholders and waiters and bakers and students and grandmothers and criminals and cabbies and tan-face girls and Rasta boys and veterans and New Punks and old Romantics and hundreds more who roar when Nikos raises the sash window. Who cheer and wave Greek flags and home-painted banners and chant the last words his father will hear:

"O-LYM-PIC! O-LYM-PIC!"
"Papa!" Nikos says over his shoulder, "I think we are back in the game."

The uninvited guest

by Alexandra Elizabeth Shine

Mark had a sickening feeling hit his stomach when he approached his front door. It was slightly ajar. He immediately thought his house had been broken into. What if they were still inside? He stopped a meter away, contemplating the possibility that maybe Mrs. Norris next door would let him use the phone to call for help. He looked around and noticed his mum's car was parked under the car port, she was home early from work. Maybe mum just left the door open? With a bravery Mark never knew he had, he crept forward and craned his neck to look into the open doorway. Strangely, nothing looked out of place, the hallway was still the same as when he left for school that morning, A wave of fear crept over him– the house as very quiet, almost too quiet.

He pushed open the door and stepped inside. The hairs on the back of his neck stood up suddenly and a chill ran down his spine – this didn't feel like house at all. There was a heaviness in the air. It was dull and ominous. He took a tentative step forward, not wanting to disturb the chilling silence. He quietly crept into the hallway – he could see his mum's keys hanging on the hall stand. He wasn't prepared to call out for her – he had this unnerving feeling that maybe there was someone else inside the house, someone who shouldn't be there. Mark could see the dust settle between the cracks of light from the window shades as the house was enveloped in a kind of darkness, one that was unsettling for four o'clock in the afternoon. He walked past the open living room doorway and could see everything was immaculate- there was no sign of a robbery. He glanced down the hallway, the kitchen door was partially closed, but it had a dodgy hinge and it never stayed open, it had been like that for years. Yet, this didn't offer his any reassurance that there was nothing to worry about.

He made his way to the staircase and looked up – the silence was deafening. His stomach was still churning and he couldn't shake this sense of foreboding. It felt like there was a haunting presence in the empty spaces around him – frightening and overpowering. He lingered at the bottom of the staircase hesitant to move any further, he was trying to decide what to do next when he heard his mother's voice call him,

"Mark, Mark! Can you come here please?" he looked toward the voice, it sounded like it was coming from her bedroom. His apprehension melted all at once; a great wave of relief washed over him and he started up the staircase. He hadn't even made it to the third step when he suddenly stopped, frozen to the spot, he had heard his mother's voice again, this time a frightful hush from behind the gaping kitchen door

"Mark, don't go up there – I heard it too."

The birdwomen of Wells-Next-The-Sea

by Ingrid Jendrzejewski

They lie in flocks on the beach, tangled amidst the seaweed, their sinewy, sun-stained bodies sprawled amidst sand and terry cloth. They watch the ships with unblinking eyes, nictating membranes twitching with the breeze that comes in from the sea. Their limbs are wet with oils, and the smells of herring and coconut emanate from their crevices.

I walk awkwardly among them, blanched, puffy, foreign. I am from a different clime, a place where the sun is weak and clouds rule supreme, a place where feet are cased in leather and briefcases are wielded as weapons. I am afraid of them, these bird women of sand and salt. When they see me, they point their sharp beaks in my direction and stare with the forward-facing eyes of birds of prey.

Offline dating

by Andy Cashmore

Today Adam will get up. He'll have a shower while the radio plays one song followed by ten minutes of adverts. He'll brush his teeth with strawberry toothpaste meant for kids and get dressed: his shirt will be untucked. As he grabs an apple on his way out, he'll put his headphones on and slam the door. This normally disturbs Adam's housemate and wakes her up. She will shout a gentle profanity in the way a kitten might scratch. Adam is unaware of this.

It's a short train journey to work. While his suitcase kisses the slender thigh of the woman next to him, Adam will contemplate his place in the world. Some days he thinks harder about it; today he wonders what his friends and family would think if they could see him. His chin creases like a hair scrunchie when he thinks this way. Adam is unaware of this.

Adam's train will stop. The doors will open to a loud machine, which moves along the platform and catches litter in a whirlwind under its body. The crowds will grunt and walk to the barrier where Adam's hand brushes the female inspector's when he shows her his ticket. Outside, broken glass belonging to a perfume vial or a beer bottle (it is undetermined) lines the road. He steps onto this glass. Adam is unaware of this.

After passing many people in suits he'll reach the office. He'll take the elevator to the fourth floor and not hear the cries of his bearded co-worker telling him to hold the doors. Adam will turn off his music and go to his desk. The computer will be switched on, but before he begins working he'll bring up the e-mail account he created last night. He'll have received no e-mails. He'll sneak a look at his profile and confirm the 'fun' picture of himself golfing isn't attractive. The bearded co-worker will linger around Adam's desk before he coughs and walks away. Adam is unaware of this.

On the way to work today, the subject, Adam, encountered four hundred and eighty-three people. Of those, three females (and one male) experienced an increased heart rate upon viewing the subject. Of the three females, one enjoys listening to the radio in the shower, pessimistic self-reflection and apples. This female is quite lonely and looking for companionship. To conclude, this female is quite compatible with the subject. Adam is unaware of this.

Shared experiences

by Aamir Kapasi

That one time we played mini-golf and the ball went in the water and we spent ten minutes trying to fish it out with our clubs. That one time we went to that Italian restaurant and you said you wouldn't let me pay because you're stubborn, but I paid anyway. That one time we were up all night watching Friends in your room and by morning we were so tired that we fell asleep and woke up at some point in the evening. That one time I was trying to finish an essay and you came over and we watched a film and I told you how annoying you were, but you knew that I was happy to see you despite what I said. That one time we sat on that bench at the local park and watched all those little kids with their whole lives in front of them and reminisced about when we were one of them. That one time we saw that awful sci-fi film at the cinema and I spent the majority of the film giggling at your reactionary facial expressions. That one time you played football with me and my friends and they all laughed at your inability to kick a ball. That one time we did coursework together and you annihilated my thesis and I had to rewrite the whole thing. That one time you were craving fish and chips and you forced me to change my clothes and leave the house and buy it for you. That one time that one bottle of wine turned into four and we became incredibly drunk and you fell asleep on the kitchen floor. That one time I was reading Nineteen Eighty-Four and you were reading Life of Pi and we spent the whole day in silence yet in unity. That one time we planned to wake up really early to eat breakfast at McDonalds, but we woke up sometime in the afternoon and we missed it. That one time we fell out because you wouldn't stop singing that cheesy song and I tried to apologise but you wouldn't accept my apology until I sang it with you. That one time we contemplated life over a coffee in the kitchen and looked out of the window and noticed how huge the sky seemed and how insignificant we were. That one time we were looking at pictures of funny faces on the internet and we laughed loudly and uncontrollably until your mother came in and told us to not wake your sister up. That one time we decided to play Come Dine With Me and I burnt our meal and we ended up ordering pizza. That one time we went for a walk by the river and that aggressive duck tried to attack us and you swore so much that people turned around and stared at us.

Yep, I think that's it. Those are all the times I've thought "I love you."

On the King's Road

by Amanda O'Callaghan

It's quiet. English department store quiet, thermostatically safe, the city blustering at the door. Today, it's all lone shoppers. We choreograph ourselves into retail's slow dance: past the new woollens, around the summer tops—marked down now—the brightest of them still looking hopeful for a last meal in the garden. We lift the latest cardigans in their dead foliage shades, sense the oncoming winter in the thick sleeves.

Suddenly, rain outside. Imported rain: tropical, unyielding. We watch the water dash itself against grey walls, pool in the hollows of the ancient road. Beside me, a woman drops an armful of coat-hangers. They skitter away like shiny, black lizards.

I think of my homeland; remember the sound of water on a tin roof, the rowdy tumble of it, cooling and cleansing. There was peace in its garrulous embrace.

But the others press towards the door, furled umbrellas poised like gearsticks. I stand beside a shelf of tall boots, their new-shape toes pointing. Perhaps it's time to leave.

Outside, the unexpected squall has moved on. A backwash of commuters silts against the bus stop. Wet collars stand to attention, hair is tamped hard to skulls. In the absence of buses, we watch the oily water carry sweet wrappers to new shores.

There are days when I am not made for all this waiting. So I wrap my neck against the freshening breeze and walk.

Halfway down the long straight, there's an old man sitting cross-legged on the damp footpath, arm held up as if testing the air for misery. I have my unused bus-fare in my hand. As I near him, I reach down to give him the coins. With a magician's dexterity he takes them, and my hand, the strength of his grip a shock, fear coming fast behind. We are locked here, on this clamouring street.

"I hope you never turn out like me," he says.

He speaks in the accent of my parents, the cadence of my past. The sound of the old country that they carried with them to nurse in a new land.

In the jolt of touching I blurt out, "No, I hope I never do." And a hectic shame rises in me.

But he nods a slow benediction, as if this could be the only answer. He shakes my hand, formally, lets it go without a word.

Today, another hot sky arcs above me. In a distant corner, afternoon clouds pile themselves into an extravagant bouffant of purple and grey. A bat wheels into the mango tree with a leafy crash. There's a storm coming.

I can never return, now, with my small bag of better words, kinder than the shaken truth I handed him that day. If I could, I would tell him that sometimes, when the rain hits the glass, predictably hard, I think of a wet-headed man on the King's Road, wishing, begging, for my salvation.

Perfection

by Courtney Button

It happens every five years. He searches across the world and chooses a girl. Hundreds apply but he only chooses one. He takes her and moulds her, shapes her in his vision. Then he displays her as the head of his new line. He is called a designer but really he is an artist and the lucky girl, she is not a model but a material, clay to shape at his will. They give their bodies and their life knowing that they become something more. He makes them more than they would ever have been.

When he is ready, he reveals them and all the world's eyes fall upon them. I've watched the unveiling since I was a very small girl. The media finds out everything about them, interviews their proud parents. Everyone wanted to be her, all parents wish their daughter would be chosen. Then we all watch the unveiling on TV. Every channel shows it, all their cameras watching. You can barely see at first because of all the flashing of the cameras but then you can see her, and she is always more beautiful than the last.

I remember the first time I saw one of his models in real life. It was the first time one of them had been open to view by the general public. The queue was huge, I waited for days. Seeing them on the television is one thing but seeing them in person is another. It was life changing. She was stood, her pose so powerful, and her look was so striking. The sight of her took my breath away. She was beautiful. No, she was more than that. She was perfection. Her skin was smooth and flawless, her teeth white and shining and her eyes so deep and full of life. She was completely still, almost from another world, a true work of art. He had taken her, an ordinary woman, and turned her in to an angel. Now she would always live on, she will be that beautiful forever. Perfectly preserved. I stared at her for hours. Up close you can see how much of a genius he is. You can see that he truly is God.

So this is why I slather myself in expensive creams, take good care of my hair, my teeth and nails. It's the reason why I spend five hours a day working out. When he sees me, he will instantly feel inspiration and only I will do. He will pick me, out of everyone else. I will give myself to him, to be his and he will take me and make me his own. He will shape me, and he will make me perfect and I will live on, beautiful forever. He will make me more than just the ordinary girl I am.

He will turn me in to an angel.

Air

by Katy Oliver

The final few days were calm. Now there were no plants, still space turned stagnant and the air turned sour because there was no wind to blow it away. It spread around the domes and became invasive, seeping through the glass and filling the cities, solid to walkthrough, and unable to satisfy the need for oxygen. The air draped heavily over the land and crushed it small, lingering and clinging to all objects, coating them in a stale film so the brain became numb and starved. Productivity was reduced and the creatures mainly slept.

It's hard to move when you're trapped on an island and everything you do is in baby steps. Resources were depleting so the governments released epidemics of lethargy that hit populations in powerful soporific clouds so the people could not tell they were losing their context. Apathy came and people grew bored; too lazy to be frustrated and drifted like overfed cats on what the governments told them they wanted. Attitudes changed and interest became redundant. Nothing mattered in these padded cells and those who had passion let it wear off and fall flat. Without anything to relate to the creatures did not feel real, so love stories happened in short bursts mimicked from old movies. We cannot be sure if they were capable of affection.

We were a useless couple. Both pretentious but hating pretention, gently catching each other out at any available opportunity. I never won because he knew more than me. I was only ever qualified on paper. He didn't watch the television on his days off, he made things out of junk he found lying around the house and listened to music I'd never heard of. He thought I was wonderful, trying to be a better person for him; self-loathing if I showed any weakness. He didn't mind when I cried it just bewildered him. We were not in love, it crossed my mind a few times, but I was unsure and I tried to only speak in certainties around him, he did not understand conflicting emotion. He was unable to get an erection for most of the time we were together and it made me feel undesirable. Sometimes I would go very deep inside myself and wish that he would not touch me, other times I ignored it. When I left, he went back to the canals and they burnt his boat. He got a disease from sleeping in the cold, they said, and died three days later. His mother told me. She rang me like a robot when I was walking through the city, going nowhere. I don't think she minded, but legislation stated it was her duty to inform the relevant people. I could not drink tea because we had none and I got a message telling me to write an obituary for the government records. I looked at the form then packed my bags. It asked me to name my three favourite things about him. I could not.

On dead dogs and crying

by Padraig O Meiscill

There is a strangely comforting sensation to feeling yourself shudder when you cry. The short, sharp gasps inwards; the long, involuntary sobs of exhalation are marked by a shaking movement that seems to be preparing your body for the repose of those who have cried their fill – releasing the last reserves of energy in a staccato burst of bone movement.

There is nothing necessarily productive or therapeutic about the act of crying uncontrollably. It doesn't resolve any issue – unless the issue at hand is impotence in the field of emitting emotions – rarely changes a person's mind and doesn't turn back any clock. Dead dogs remain dead, no matter how long we cry for them.

But it undoubtedly settles us, if only to put us more comfortably at ease with our melancholy.

I remember, through stained eyes, the protruding stomach of my grandfather shrouded in thick, rough wool as a comforting hand pulled me closer to his chest. The shudders reverberate as if off walls when someone holds you tight like that.

In the small, rectangular hall that opened onto the back garden where the dog lay dead, there were peeled potato skins on the floor, the rudimentary scribbles of children on the walls and the low hum of the refrigerator behind us.

Through the double window of the back door, pink vomit, reminiscent of melted ice cream discarded by a child on a hot summer day, could be seen surrounding the dog's head, at rest on the dirty grey flagstone.

He retained a quiet dignity in death, minus the vomit. Legs in pairs, outstretched, not sprawled. Mouth firmly shut, no tongue hanging low, gasping for that last drop of water or air. The dog shit that littered the back yard was of a different day and retained that dignified distance from the canine lying in state. Who knows, maybe he chose his spot of death on the very basis that he'd used everywhere else as a toilet.

His rough, red hair gave him, to my mind, the look of a warrior laid low. In hindsight, he was frail, skinny and sick to the point of expiry, while the red was turning a scruffy brown.

There are moments now implanted whose recall is only possible through poetic license. Of rambles on a mountainside with the dog, or was it us, in tow. Of dishes of cold stout for the dog, pints of it for the grandfather and a coke for the kid. Of hanging with abandon to the dog's back while he ran in circles in a desperate canter for freedom. Of a dog rabid with the rest of the world and gentle only with me.

I cried for all these things. I cried because it was winter and raining and my school uniform was covered in my snot. I cried for a grandfather as sick as the dog but not yet as tired of living.

I cried to be still and, by measures, it came.

My hands

by Jacqueline Winn

I am not my hands, though I have to say they're good at what they do. I can fill a thousand bottles of shampoo in an hour, screw down as many caps and have the lot packed in boxes faster than anyone else in the whole factory. Anywhere on the line, my hands are the best. I suspect my hands are all you see but, let me tell you, my eyes, my ears, my mind are all just as good. And my voice, if you could hear me sing above the din, is even better. But how could you know? Bundy in, feed the line, bundy out. That's all you need, my hands.

Right now, they're in my lap, not knowing what to do. They fidget and grip, twine and grasp. At straws. Hoping, against all evidence to the contrary, that it's not what I fear behind that office door.

To my left are a dozen just like me. Hands in laps, grasping. All called in from the line when they shut off the power just before morning break.

"That's it," the line supervisor yelled, as the electrics ground down, the rollers squeaked to a halt. "Everyone on lines C, D and E, off to management."

Before she marched off, she slapped the last of the packed boxes. Once they've sold, there'll be a sign in the supermarket: line discontinued.

When I first sat down in this chilly corridor, I was in the middle. But now to my right there are six empty seats. They haven't come back, those women. That's because behind that office door is a desk and a manager, and behind him another door. The quick exit door, a concession to shame and tears that don't care to be carried through the factory floor.

"Next!"

I hesitate a moment to throw a silly smile of never mind along the row of women I've seen every day for fifteen years. And a little flutter of my hand. It will have to do for goodbye. A few return the courtesy.

Once in the office, I press my hands against the door and close it behind me. He gestures to the chair, but I'll remain standing. It's a small attempt at dignity he can't possibly imagine. My hands, that's all he sees. The hands that have paid his wage, kept his office. The hands that take the dismissal letter and tremble as I murmur a ridiculous, "Thank you."

Walking out into the quiet sunshine, I hum a little. Things could be worse but I'm not sure how. I hum a little louder. There are lots of things I could do but I can't think what. So I hum even louder. But then the dreadful silence slaps me full in the face and a throttled sob blurts out from nowhere. My hands clasp my mouth and tears begin to soak the crumpled dismissal. And all I can think is; I am my hands.

Recollections

by Patrick Pye

I remember the pattern of the carpet. Brown diamonds interspersed with pale spots, surrounded by fading yellow. It had grown thin with age. The couch on the other hand was new and soft; plain red, well-fluffed cushions. My dad was sitting on it in his usual place, directly opposite the television set that stood in the corner of the room. On the wall to its right were shelves, stacked with books, above the sideboard, which sported a variety of pictures and ornaments. To its left, the window. The blinds were drawn.

I remember one ornament in particular, because it had my name on it. A clay rocking-horse made by a family friend. It used to watch us as we watched the TV, which, for a change, was off. The remote control was in the middle of the floor. So were two of the well-fluffed, plain red cushions.

I remember some of the pictures on the sideboard. There was one of my parents on their wedding day, and one of me, making my first holy communion. I was wearing a red tie and had my hands together, as if I was praying. There was another, of all three of us in Cornwall, taken when I was only two. We were on the beach. The sea was in the background.

I remember that there was a wooden crucifix on the wall, dozens of folded crosses stuffed behind it, collected over a series of Palm Sundays. The ironing board was up, as it usually was. Clothes were piled all over it, as they usually were. The door to the kitchen was slightly ajar; as was the door I had just come through. My fingers still touched the handle.

I remember dad calling my name, then hurrying down the stairs. I remember the placement of the cushions, the clothes, the strange quiet and the way he was facing away from me as I entered. I remember that he still had the beard, and his bald patch was yet to fully materialise. He would have been wearing slippers. He always wore slippers indoors.

What I don't remember is his facial expression, his tone of voice, or the exact words he used to tell me that mum was dead. I just remember closing the door behind me and hurrying back up the stairs.

Tabula rasa

by Cathy Lennon

Jenny's kitchen table was made of wood so heavy you could hardly move it. Ours came out of a cardboard box and was put together with a screwdriver. Even the scars on Jenny's table looked good. If there had been any cracks in the veneer on ours, all you'd see would be fibres of glued grey pulp.

Jenny's kitchen table was always cluttered and becrumbed. There'd be a jug of wildflowers sometimes, a chrome cafetière, a wine cork, piles of sheet music scattered with clarinet reeds. At one end there'd be a stack of multi-section newspapers and magazines displaying artful ornaments and country views. Ours was pristine, a fruit bowl on a faux lace mat.

I did my homework at school, on buses, in the public library, in bed at night. I never brought people home. Jenny did her homework at the kitchen table while her mother swigged wine and leaned against the aga and talked about poets. 'What do you think?' Jenny's mum would ask me, not so sparkly though, out of politeness. Jenny's father would come in, snaffle olives or a gulp of wine, roll his eyes, offer me a lift home.

Jenny's university place letter lay on her kitchen table for weeks, casually accumulating coffee cup rings on its historic coat of arms. Mine was carefully folded into its envelope and put into a drawer, pulled out fearfully, for anxious exchanges that involved a calculator and lots of forms. At Jenny's results party, the table top bristled with bottles and glasses and Jenny's Labrador hid underneath, watching. I wanted to stay there forever if I could, this place where doors opened wide onto a sunlit lawn.

They came to one of my tables, one evening, Jenny's mum and dad. They didn't know I worked here now. 'How's uni?' she said in that old, polite way. 'Clever of you choosing to study here, so you still have all your home comforts.' I smiled and gave them each a menu, rattled off the specials.

She tried again, when I brought them the bill. 'We miss the old days, all of you round the kitchen table.' I looked at him then, Jenny's dad, and he looked away. For a moment I was tempted to say it, that I miss that kitchen table too. It was so solid against my back, unmoving despite our exertions, the flowers just inches from my ear, the glossy magazines sliding to the floor, my eyes widening in joy, drinking it all in, him in me and this wonderful world of possibility.

After they left I took out my phone. Jenny had uploaded more pictures from her May Ball. A message came in from mum, asking me to get formula milk on the way home. I took a cloth to the black lacquered table top. 'Steady on,' joked my boss. 'Or you'll have all the shine off it.' I just kept on trying to wipe it clean.

Heat death

by Ingrid Jendrzejewski

"I never know if this helps," she says. She is fanning herself with Great Expectations. "It feels nice, but I'm using energy, aren't I?"

I nod faintly, making the smallest possible movement in acknowledgement. Yes, yes you are using energy. I don't speak the words, though; her fanning cools me too, and I like the feel of the breeze.

"The same with electric fans. I can't sleep at night without one, but all it's doing is moving air around, right? And burning energy. Sucking it out of the walls. Turning electricity into heat. Why does it feel so cool, when it's actually making everything hotter?"

I let the side of my mouth twitch, hoping she finds it a sufficient response. She can go on like this for ages and I am tired.

"I mean, I'm okay with air conditioners. They make things cooler in one place but hotter in another. That I can understand. As long as I'm in the cool place, I'm happy. But fans… they just don't make sense." She lapses into silence, like a capacitor pausing to charge before its next explosive release. In her quiet, she glances at me. The book continues to flutter in her hand.

I could explain about sweat and evaporation, about how the movement of air increases convective heat loss. Wind chill. Thermodynamics. About the amount of energy required to power a fan, about the caloric requirement to power the waving of an arm. I could save myself seconds or minutes or hours of her aimless musings. I could tell her things that, I believe, she would genuinely find interesting. I could do all these things. But I don't. It is a hot summer and I already know that our two thermal bodies won't be sharing the same heat reservoir for long. We are already cooling, and at such a rate that I know it's not efficient to spend any more energy trying to keep the flame alive.

As her hand stills and a bead of perspiration meanders down the side of her face, I wonder if maybe we would have lasted longer if the summer hadn't been so hot, or if I didn't know so much about entropy.

Cenotaph

by Karen Lethlean

By the time mourners had gathered and were milling about on the beach, the swell mellowed as if to suit the sombre occasion. Many had already shed tears; but still shook each other's hands warmly and commented on how much they missed old Joe. On some unspoken signal, they took to their boards and paddled out oblivious to this bejewelled ocean.

Past the breakers, they formed a circle. Safe, where the swell won't force them onto the rocky ends of this narrow cove. Here there was limited beach sand to soften any edges; instead this shoreline was strewn with black volcanic boulders, like so many others. Even though only early afternoon, the sky had turned grey again with Vog*.

No one moved toward a sensual wave that promised a ride tinged with danger, its curve enough to send a rider tumbling over the small reef towards ominous dark fringe beyond ready to pummel and crush. Most of the mourners had already encountered variant limb to rock collisions.

As if respecting Joe's life stillness settled. Crashing shore waves dimed to background hum. Even ceaseless breezes paused. Everyone straddled boards as if these craft were extensions of limbs, even though this surfing heritage had killed Joe.

Troy began a prayer; others bowed heads, eyes half closed to capture whatever individual image of their passed friend each felt necessary.

From a red tub Robbie threw flowers. Plumeria, broad petal frangipani in pink, yellow and cream, star shaped island Gardenia, Marigolds; these were all scattered, and then settled within the circle like confetti. Next, he emptied the ashes. These made a grey net on the water's surface; from the beach a long sombre note on a conch shell was blown; four times, for each direction. Board riders scooped handfuls of ocean and sprinkled back ripples like holy water. But this didn't disturb the cradle of grey and flower dapples that waited for one last thing. Beginning with Al everyone dived from their boards and washed themselves in Joe's remains; then surfaced within the last few tangible elements that had been their friend.

Below the water, they could each feel how Joe would have touched – a kiss for her; a poke in the ribs to him; a reassuring hand on the shoulder there. Unwilling to break away, disappointed that this remembrance was the only reason they were here, each remained within the circle treading water.

Even without leg ropes their boards did not stray but remained in formation as if reverence for Joe was deeper than tide, currents and drift.

As is inevitable, break away they must, but not by paddling to the shore. Each took a wave in Joe's honour. Something pushed these surfers even though many waves were taken through misted tears.

Robbie remained the longest, well after dusk had settled into real dark, riding on, one last wave, one more time for Joe.

Vog is volcanic fog that settles like cloud cover blowing northward from Kilauea's plume.

The reliable witness

by Sandra Crook

The years have been kind to him; kinder than they have to me.

On this chilly January day, he's enjoying his moment in the flicker of flash photography, the clamour of people seeking his views; it's been a long time.

He turns his head this way and that, as though each posture has been rehearsed carefully before a triple-view mirror. There's an almost languorous air to every movement; even his eyelids droop slowly with every well-choreographed blink, opening just as slowly to reveal ice-blue eyes that have mesmerised men and women alike over the years.

His wife is a study in contrasts. Her movements are jerky, almost bird-like, her glittering eyes constantly surveying the crowd. That perfectly reconstructed jaw is clenched, and a tiny pulse flickers beneath her ear. She stands erect, proud and clad, probably on his advice, in faux fur. He has an instinct for the ebb and flow of public opinion, a talent that's served them both well over recent weeks.

"Could you tell us how you feel, now it's all over," calls a television reporter, as fur-muffled microphones are thrust forward.

He pauses for effect.

"I feel..." There is a long pause. I wonder whether some of the journalists aren't shifting impatiently, glancing towards the doors of the courthouse, looking for other, speedier fish to fry.

".... exonerated, saddened..."

He pauses again, and a journalist, impatient for a sound-bite, prompts him.

"Relieved?"

I see the flash of irritation, just as quickly concealed.

"Relieved? I was innocent, so I feel no relief... only total vindication, and a sense that justice has prevailed."

For a moment, it seems he might not be asked to elaborate on these sentiments, yet I know he'll do so, even if some gullible acolyte does not oblige.

He takes a deep breath. "There are no victors, in these cases. Everyone, young or old, rich or poor, is a victim."

He glances towards a taxi which has just pulled up, and into which the three hunched and snivelling prosecution witnesses are being ushered, all trembling lips and trickling mascara. His mood switches rapidly and he pulls his shoulders back; he always had a low threshold for martyrdom.

"It's been a witch-hunt, unreliable witnesses... all of them, just as the judge said. Foolish women whc..."

I see, though I doubt others will, the light pressure his wife's hand exerts on his elbow, and the slight shifting of her position.

"... *unfortunate* women who..."

I take one step forward from the crowd and he stops, mid-oratory. His wife looks puzzled.

His eyes meet mine, and the snap of recognition is instantaneous.

I hadn't intended to do this. Indeed, I've been resolute in the face of pleas, persuasion, coercion and appeals to a better nature I no longer possess.

I may regret this tomorrow, but at this moment, as eloquence deserts him, I feel the deepest thrill of satisfaction.

Because suddenly he's old, so very, very old.

And I was so young; so impossibly young back then.

Haunting

by Alice Cairns and Mary Trend

Her brother was a pale boy with an easy, sudden smile, adored from the day he was born. In truth, she was little more than an afterthought to parents, content to have produced so satisfactory an heir. But she never resented Arthur, her playmate and her friend. It was his voice, his laughter, his footsteps that filled the house and made it live. All her life she had known that he would inherit the house, buying back the land they had been forced to sell and repairing the crumbling plasterwork.

Then had come the telegram, and after that there was no brother, no heir, only a corpse in a British Army hospital somewhere north of Flanders. The house would see no more children. Instead an oppressive quiet had settled over the place like fine dust that she did not know how to lift, never having learnt the knack.

She supposed it was Arthur's empty place at breakfast that had decided her Father. The land was sold to developers and would become a picturesque suburb. The house itself was of no use to anybody. Its antiques would be sold, its panelling stripped, its most pleasing interiors transported piece by piece to America. Its tremendous carcass was promised to a demolition contractor.

As the house emptied, the memory of Arthur seemed to fill up more space. It was he who would chase her down corridors, who would give the sombre portraits silly voices, would sit with her in the spinney at midnight and listen to the owls. He had told her about the ghost. A woman in white – a nun, perhaps, or a bride - who would walk the Gallery at night, weeping. When they were young, they had crept from their beds in the dark and waited, their hearts pumping, their sweaty hands clasped, in the hope of seeing her. They never had.

On an impulse, she stood, the air chill against the thin cotton of her pale nightgown, and walked to the Gallery. She was taken aback, momentarily, by the brightness of the room. Propped against the walls were all the mirrors of the house, stored to be auctioned. Twenty or thirty priceless pieces leaning haphazardly against each other. They caught and refracted the moonlight until the whole room was eerily bright. The mirrors were old, tarnished, in heavy frames of Venetian gilt and Tudor wood. Foxing silvered the glass in a mist, as though someone had breathed on it moments before.

Each of the mirrors reflected back a room without Arthur, but in every one stood a woman in white, weeping.

Snowslip

by Emma J Myatt

On Sunday evening, he doesn't come home. The climbers' forecast that morning had warned her: strong winds, blizzard conditions on higher ground. She sends a whispered prayer north to the mountains. She paces the lounge. Impatience rushes her to burn dinner - which she can hardly eat - scald her tongue on coffee, take a yowling step on the cat.

Through the window she looks into darkness and tries his phone again, imagining him digging his way out of an avalanche to get to her. At ten o'clock she calls mountain rescue and describes his clothing and tent to the tiniest detail. Even the colour of his socks. She shudders as she says, *red gloves*, seeing cold blue hands inside. She imagines that strength, dead.

She takes a pill and tries to sleep, the phone next to her pillow. It's a fitful sleep full of cold white dreams in which she's sledging, terrifyingly fast and free, the wind howling wildness in her head.

There's no news on Monday despite helicopters circling clear skies; rescuers scouring the tracks. Neighbours come, sympathy in their eyes as they take in her sloppy clothes and her tense, stripped face.

On Tuesday afternoon, she takes a cardboard box from the attic and packs some of his things, just to see what it feels like. She's writing **Red Cross** on it in pink pen when the phone rings.

Once she's replaced all his possessions, she stumbles up the stairs and paints her face with shaking hands. She dresses properly. Whilst making dinner she practises her smile.

Tepoztlán

by Sofia Falomir

It was deep into the night. The roof terrace where we stood seemed to stretch far out into the blackness. The silhouettes of the town spread below us; a small town in a valley in Mexico, with its cobbled roads, the paint peeling off the otherwise bright-coloured houses, and the barking of dogs in the distance, coming from somewhere along the road that reached towards the mountains.

Below us was the glimmering street; above was the night sky; ahead, the looming mountains. A lamppost stood beneath us on our right, shyly casting its frail beams, most of which got lost in darkness. A few tenacious flakes of light managed to cling to the individual cobbles of the road, and to the protuberances of the bricks on the wall opposite. It created a small picture of light that hung with invisible, frail nails amid the imperturbable night, as a painting on an endless wall of blackness. A cat jumped in to the luminous halo, reared its head, then left.

Some beams of light rested as a thin thread on the banister of the terrace that would have otherwise merged with the hues of the mountains that ominously stood ahead. The landscape seemed to sway and quiver, ever so slightly. Everything had a pulse, and somehow seemed endowed with life. I had only to fix my gaze on something — a light coming out of the houses at the skirts of the mountains — and it would start breathing, speaking to me of meanings that I could not, perhaps needed not, understand.

My gaze traced the silhouettes of a tree in the distance, which seemed to speak of nature, of leaves, of life, of death, of branches. All was patterns, all was meaning. The light meant a household, meant a family, meant people; it meant consciousness's as intricate and ineffable as mine. Everything around me was a portal to a never-ending rabbit-hole. The tree sunk under its own weight, and so did the light. The dark surfaces of the landscape opened pores of further darkness. One needed only to follow one of the paths deep enough, and be lost.

And so we stood, holding on tight to each other. Silently

refusing to step out of the two tiles on the floor that had become a small island, or a piece of driftwood, the only shelter from the void that surrounded us and tried to swallow me whole; all those eternal, bottomless tunnels, of vertiginous emptiness and irresistible sway. They drew me in, and I had to hold tight; to you, and to my tiny, frail spot in the unfathomable, voracious universe.

But it was still beautiful. The night of the magnifying glass, you would later call it. The night we held a magnifying glass into the chasms of the night.

Every day

by Kerry Hood

Every day, she dresses before sun is up; boils chai; scoops yesterday's dhal onto a roti. Next, she takes a bottle of yellow oil and kneads it into her forehead and shrivelled lobe, the greedy skin sucking salve into its corrugations, lapping the lips and tight space below her nose. Amina is thirty-two.

Every day she walks through the empty compound, feeling her two sons asleep over the wall of the second enclosure and hearing an old man hurl spit across the grain earth. Every day Amina is sent to the airport. She rides a blue-smoke moped. She pretends it's a bicycle. She lifts her feet and speeds down Red Dust Road past plastic bags breathing with flat striped lungs in the ditches.

She zoooooooooooooooms........................ along the villas in the Portuguese Quarter, feeling through her closed lids the blade shadows of their shutters.

In the real world she must keep an eye open. She stands at Departures, one hand held out, the other making a hunger sign. She does this because she was once disobedient then punished by her husband and mother-in-law with a colourless liquid. Her right eye is burned away. Pleated rinds of scar tissue make it impossible to smile, as if she would with her children hidden from her. They believe she is dead. Every day Amina puts an ear to her tiny window and hears them running breath-heavy from bully cousins. She beats her own head knowing they'll forget her.

Only, *this* day she's still in her room, the yellow oil a glassy lake on her face. She's listening for the exact silence that means it's safe. Shushing herself, she treads across the compound. Soon she's pushing the moped along the road. She's not going to the airport. The sun is almost up. She must hurry. She has stolen her children.

She's been planning for a month, since the airport worker had folded the note onto her palm. (Lately, porters and cleaners had been staring at Amina, whispering in packs). Now they suddenly appeared, moving forward from all sides. She panicked. Dropped the note. Saw it was an address for Women's Refuge. Knew it would be impossible. She was on her knees. Someone brought her to her feet. The workers began filing past, smiling, filling Amina's hands until – despite her baldness – she let down her headscarf to catch fountains of notes, coins, messages of luck.

The eldest sits behind Amina on the moped, his arms binding her ribs. The little one is on her lap gripping her sari in his fists. All are open-mouthed, afraid, complete. The little one turns to stare at Amina. He traces the ruts from eye socket to throat; lifts the corners of her defaced mouth. The eldest stretches up to her ear.

"We will have every day!" he shouts over the throttle. "Every day, mumma!"

Amina nods. There will be every day to practise but just now she tries, oh she really tries, to do her first beautiful smile.

Three chords and the truth

by Steven Holding

"One Two Three Four!"

They tear into the song, furiously attacking the track, tightly embracing the slight acceleration in tempo that live performance always seems to bring to the piece. He hangs limply off the mic stand, nodding head crammed to capacity with the throb of bass and drums. The shit in his bloodstream is certainly doing its thing as he howls his way through garbled lyrics, eager for the number to be over and done with.

The hungry crowd are devouring every frenzied second of the blistering set. Rapturous applause rattles his bones; shrieks and wolf whistles signalling the shared climax of the tune's abrupt conclusion.

The band strike a chord. Another melody commences. His voice rises as the verse expands, words and music merging. Next, the seamless shift into the uplifting chorus. As the sea of faces singalong, shuttered eyes block out all of those who have come to worship. A rush, a push and he is finally cut loose. Lost in the momentum of the moment, blindly searching for the beating heart that hides somewhere within the lines.

Looking to get back to the split second where everything began.

Somewhere, a fresh-faced youth picks at the strings of his bruised guitar, plucking words from the ether with nonchalant ease, scrawling the rhymes in blood red biro on the dog-eared pages of a spiral bound notebook. As the vowels and consonants intermingle with a pleasingly simple arpeggio, his only concern is to capture the purity of that which flows through his soul then share it with the beauty who ignites such a powerful flame, using the only way he knows how.

As the masses chant in unison, he falls back into the now, wondering, as always, what the boy would make of this; of how something so fragile and fleeting has ended up meaning so much to so many.

It's a mystery.

He gazes out, squinting into the sweltering light, studying those who watch him.

She's not there of course, he knows that she never will be, but still, there is always hope.

Until a single teardrop mixes with the sweat, making him flinch as he remembers once again. The sudden realisation, the terrifying shame, shivering as he admits that he can no longer distinguish any of them from the hazy distant memory of her face.

Reminding himself that he cannot even recall her name.

Scratched enamel heart

by Amanda Huggins

Alice wore a bracelet to commemorate the dead. The bracelet was made from plaited leather that wrapped twice around her wrist, stained with sweat and chlorine and soap, strung with heavy silver charms; the weight of those she'd lost.

She wore it all the time, and the charms dug into her wrist in the night and clattered against her desk during the day. She fingered the maneki-neko with its scratched enamel heart, the squat owl with its missing green glass eye, and the dented cross-legged Buddha. Year after year she carried them around on a darkening ribbon of cow hide; these semi-precious mementos of her parents and her baby. She kept them where she could see them; as a comfort, not a reminder. She didn't need reminders. Every morning, grief punched her from the inside. It reared up with tiny pointed teeth, rammed into her like concrete, always re-settling at the heart of her; a dense sediment, waiting to be shaken up by a child's laughter, the chime of the church clock, or the heady scent of wallflowers.

Her new therapist, Olivia, wore a bracelet too. It was rose gold and strung with Venetian glass beads and enamelled charms: unicorns, seahorses and flowers. She twisted it absentmindedly around her slender, tanned wrist, and when she lifted her hand to tuck her hair behind her ear, Alice noticed the Tiffany logo on the clasp. And she could tell, without asking, that Olivia hadn't lost anyone yet.

The visitor

by James McKenzie Watson

Wilma approaches a rotund woman with a kind face who's handing jelly cups out to the residents. The woman smiles, her badge identifying her as *Rhonda – RN.*

"Hello, Wilma. How are you?"

"Well, thank you. Where's Jean?"

"In the living room, love."

Past the bedrooms, through the forest of dining tables surfaced with beige lyonium. Jean's asleep in an armchair, her lips flapping as she snores. Wilma takes the chair beside her. *The Sound of Music* is on TV. None of the glassy-eyed residents seem interested in it.

Jean stirs and notices Wilma with a frown.

"How long have you been here?"

"Not long. I didn't want to wake you."

They watch *The Sound of Music* together. Rhonda offers them each a cup of tea. They both decline.

"What do I do after this?" Jean finally says.

"What do you mean?"

"What do I do? Do I have dinner? Do I go to bed?"

"You don't have to do anything. You can just sit here and watch telly."

Jean sighs. "I want to go home. This isn't home."

"I know," says Wilma. "But they're looking after you. They're keeping you safe."

"I don't want to be safe. I want to be home." There's pain in her pale eyes. "Isn't that what you want too?"

Julie Andrews starts up again. Jean nods back off to sleep.

Rhonda's doing paperwork in the office as Wilma heads for the exit. The unit is like a maze. Down endless halls, past endless rooms. Eventually, Wilma finds herself back outside Rhonda's office.

"You alright, Wilma?" says Rhonda.

"Yes. I can just never remember how to get out."

"Oh, I know, it's a labyrinth, isn't it? The traffic's shocking this afternoon anyway, maybe you should stay till the worst is over."

Wilma pauses. "Maybe that's not a bad idea, yes."

She sits back next to Jean and watches the world outside darken. She stands again as Rhonda sets gelatinous roast dinners on the tables.

"I probably should be off now," says Wilma. "It's getting dark."

"Are you sure?" says Rhonda. "You're welcome to stay for dinner."

Wilma looks at the shimmering glop. "Do you make spare meals?"

"We've already got one for you. Over there, next to Jean's." She gestures to a table in the corner. Two meals side-by-side.

"But if I stay much longer, I'll have to stay the night," Wilma says with a laugh.

"That's okay, we've already got a room all made up for you."

"Really?"

"Yes."

"What, just for me?"

"Just for you, love."

The residents are shuffling to the tables where they're given bibs and helped to sit. It strikes Wilma with profound weight. She looks to Rhonda whose warm smile is now sad. She understands. The grief rises in Wilma's chest like a bubble, new and familiar all at once.

"Go on, sweet," says Rhonda. "Go and get started on your dinner. Your friend will be missing you."

Wilma sits beside Jean. Julie Andrews is still singing.

The elephant in the room

by Xanthe Knox

Thomas Willows had spent the first twelve hours in the waiting room of the afterlife equal parts confused and angry. The Elephant that had killed him sat on an oversized chair on the opposite wall, glaring at him.

"Does he have to be here?" he'd asked the red-haired receptionist behind the front desk. "He did trample me to death."

To Thomas's surprise the Elephant had replied, "You shot me first. Busted my head open."

The woman shrugged. "You both died together. Makes sense you're here together. Why don't you read a magazine until Saint Pete is ready to see you?"

Thomas didn't want to read a magazine. Thomas didn't want to be dead. And if he absolutely had to be dead, he didn't want to be stuck in a room with the Elephant he'd killed, which had also killed him.

He leaned in over the desk and lowered his voice to a whisper.

"The thing is, I didn't know animals made it up here. I mean, I've shot quite a few of them if I'm being honest. What's that going to mean for me..." he pointed to the door labelled *Saint Peter*, "...in there with him?"

By way of reply, the woman leaned forward and tapped a laminated sign on the counter which read: *Please do not ask reception questions regarding likelihood of being admitted into Heaven. Thank you for your understanding.*

Frowning, Thomas returned to his seat across from the Elephant who seemed to be glaring even harder.

Reluctantly, Thomas picked up one of the magazines and skimmed over an article on Elvis and Anne Boleyn's recent wedding.

"Bit worried, are you?"

The Elephant was talking to him again. He decided to ignore it. Guest list included Cleopatra and Marilyn Monroe.

"I can't imagine they usually let first degree murderers in, can you? Suspect that's probably a key prohibiting factor."

"Well you killed me too!" Thomas spat back.

"I was defending myself mate."

"I'm higher up on the food chain. It's natural."

"You think they're big on evolution-based arguments up here?"

Thomas lifted the magazine in front of his face to block the view between them. Stephen Hawking had been noticeably absent at the nuptials.

The clock on the wall above him chimed three o'clock, and the receptionist called out, "Abdu. Saint Peter will see you now."

As Abdu opened the door with his trunk, the light which emerged blinded Thomas for the few seconds it took the Elephant to pass through and click it shut again behind him.

An age seemed to pass. Half-an-hour to be exact. But what was time in this place? Was his body still lying amongst the trees in Zimbabwe? Had they found him? Did his family know?

As the clock struck four, the red-haired woman looked up from her typewriter and called, "In you go Mister Willows, Saint Peter will see you now."

A jog

by Tom Moody

You always try to run at lunchtime and today you plan to run on the long sands. She says she needs the exercise too, so can she tag along? You are pleased, flattered she'd seek your company. It's only a five-minute drive and you both change before you set off. She has brought shorts and T shirt with her today. As she climbs into the passenger seat you become aware of how well-muscled her thighs are in her black, Lycra shorts. She has told you she still occasionally rides horses. She has a good "seat".

You park at the sea front, lock the car and set off along the sands. The wind is against you and it's colder than you thought but you carry on. You'll soon warm up, you think. It's hard-going on the soft, dry sand so you slant towards the tideline where the surface is damp and firm. The wind begins to pick up threads of sand and send them swirling across your path. She jogs on your shoulder, easily matching your pace. She smiles as you glance across.

A dark shadow runs toward you along the sands. The sunshine disappears. Out of nowhere clouds have piled up over the ruined abbey on the headland. The first drops of rain touch your face. Those few drops quickly become a shower. The wind increases, and the spring rain is suddenly mixed with hail, stinging your face and arms. You turn to look at her, her eyes are narrowed against the weather. She is keeping pace, but she is no longer smiling. Someone has to say it and it's you.

"This is crazy. Let's turn back!"

Thankfully, she nods in agreement. You run faster as you return to the car. The wind hurrying you along. You release the door locks and you both tumbled into the calm. Both of you are breathing hard with the effort. Your combined breath and your wet clothing quickly cause the windows to mist up. You look at each other and laugh, relieved to be out of the wind. You turn to her.

"What were we thinking of?"

She half-turns toward you. Her pageboy hair has flattened into a damp helmet, making her look younger, more vulnerable, than ever. Her lips are parted, face flushed. You are aware of how her damp T shirt clings to her small breasts, her flat belly. You look into each other's eyes. You are so close, just centimetres between your lips. You feel her breath against your face. The air is charged, your skin prickles.

You can feel two futures diverge from this point. Like some parallel universe, two lives go on from this moment. One completely altered, remade from just one contact. The other runs in its old groove; wife, kids, mortgage? You fail to move.

The choice has been made. You start the engine; stare through the clearing the screen. You shake your head like you've just woken up and say again.

"What were we thinking of?"

The unexpected arrival of the black guy

by Charlotte Josephs

When I told him I'd chosen him as the character in a story, he chuckled and dug his fingers into his bush-like hair. I could feel his right leg vibrating against the table, sending splashes of my tea onto the wooden surface.

"Call it the unexpected arrival of the black guy," he said.

The sun had painted the sky orange and pink with wisps of white cloud when Laura's trip back to the University of East Anglia began. The walk to the train station wasn't a particularly long one, but that day it seemed to take hours. Laura's travel case weighed a ton, and even with the two of us dragging it, the twenty-minute walk was verging on forty.

"Fucking shitty wheels. Waste of money, this case," she cursed as we dragged it over the icy ground. The case groaned in response; a gritty ripping sound that tore through my eardrums and made me cringe. We were silent for a while, as the frosty wind ripped through our coats and scratched at our skin. Pulling my scarf up over my face, I grunted and forced myself through the wind. The case gripped the earth as we heaved it up the curb and we heard a pop. The second wheel had broken, and my right arm was beginning to ache with the strain. By the time we reached the station, I'd switched arms more times than I could remember.

"I can't believe I'm not gonna see our Gaz for six months and he hasn't even come to say bye," Laura sighed as we waited on platform one. The train left in ten minutes. "He just sent me a text asking where we are. I told him what time my train was at yesterday. He's at ours."

I sighed "That's shit" – and it was. We're pretty close, the three of us. We even bought each other the exact same Christmas presents, just in different colours – you know the saying, great minds.

The sky grasped our attention as we waited. Stars were beginning to crawl into sight as orange faded to blue. It matched my mood as the clock counted down to the departure of my twin. Looking over to her, I saw that she was as miserable as me. She looked up and shrugged at me in understanding. We went back to watching the stars. The train waiting at the red light when we heard him.

"LAURRRAAA," he called in his classic Tarzan expression. His brown afro bobbed up and down as he ran, flailing his arms and legs in the air like a clown. It was clear by the colour of his face – red, rather than his natural caramel brown – and the heaving of his breath that he'd run the entire way down from our house.

"Bet you didn't expect to see me here."

The list

by Kathryn Clark

I wake with the taste of burnt cabbage in my mouth. I never sleep in the day. It must be the tablets. The world outside has been silenced by snow. Here, in the house, the light is pale green. It's like waking under water.

I look at the clock. Time to go to school. I fill my pockets with spare gloves and miniature chocolate bars.

Cutting up the snicket and across the field, the snow goes over my ankles. Mine are the only footprints. No one else has walked this way. When I get to the lane an old Land Rover rumbles ahead, churning the snow to porridge.

At the school gate, I stop. The playground is crowded with snowmen, staring with stony eyes. The home-time hum is starting up. Parents coming to pick up their children pass by me with eyes turned away. I shouldn't have come.

"Laura! Laura!" Sandy's calling out to me. She's waving as if we've arranged to meet. Swathed in a pink and red shawl, she's like an exotic flower against the heavy sky. She hugs me; stands with her gloved fingers on my cheeks, like a lover staring into my eyes.

We start to walk.

"Look at the snowmen," she says. "Aren't they amazing?"

I nod, but they scare me, frozen there, doing nothing, stuck, unable to move until they melt away into nothing.

We bribe her boys with chocolate to come away from the snowball battle. They're flagging anyway, faces sore from snow and snot.

Benji, the youngest, accepts my offer of dry gloves; then puts his hand in mine. At his touch an arrow shoots up my arm and into my heart.

"These are Jem's gloves," he says.

I nod.

"Where is he?" he asks.

"He's with his Dad," I say.

"Do they live with their Dad now, him and Meena?"

"They're sort of on holiday."

"They're missing all the snow," says Benji.

Sandy makes tea while I sit at her kitchen table. Her "to-do" list sits in front of me. I remember it, the list. In the middle between phone plumber, Freddie new trainers, workshop plan, nit lotion, tax return, I see my name, highlighted, starred, underlined. I take up her pen and cross me out.

I haven't written a list for months. No need, once there was only me, once everyone was gone. Nothing I had to remember, except to take the tablets.

I flip over the page to a new sheet and write:

To do list:

1.   Get my children back

A liminal world

by Jennifer Gyrzenhout

An orange half-light pokes through the tent flap turning the inside aglow. He slides a lumpy red sleeping bag over our unclothed bodies, and the two colours twist and clash into a yolky dome above us. The flap flutters with each puff of air as we cavort zealously. Utter chaos. Some coalition of nervousness and longing, of the cool draft seeping in from outside, vying with the hot air inside, of being on the cusp of discovery in this liminal world of tangled limbs and joints. His name is Richard and his breath plays a terse tune like that of a trumpet against the point where my neck meets my shoulder. I move my legs in time, like an awkward child learning to dance on a crooked stage, haphazardly spinning pirouettes and fumbling for balance. The crickets chirp from behind the wings and the leaves in the trees rustle appreciatively.

Afterwards we sit outside gulping at the fresh, cool air, holding hands. We watch the fronds of grass whisper as frogs jump and croak in the enigmatic night. We've conquered a mountain, discovered a secret hidden in the depths of the deepest, darkest sea, a treasure trapped inside a treasure chest and only we have the key. We think not of permanence but only of the moment as delicious as every juicy drop of a bright red strawberry on our tongues in the hot summer.

It is a good thing we do not yet know how quickly it will fade.

Looks

by Chris Connolly

You look at her sitting there on the steel bench on the platform, trying not to look like you're looking but hoping she looks up and notices you looking and looks back at you in the same way. She looks good – more importantly she has that look about her – and you hope you're looking good today too, but it's been a long day and it's windy – your hair must be all over the place – so you look at your reflection in your phone, then look stealthily around to make sure no one is watching as you fix the stray hairs and hope they stay fixed.

You keep looking over, but she's absorbed in a magazine – It's called 'Look', one of those glossy magazines that have celebrities on the cover looking either too fat or too skinny. You think she has the balance between too fat and too skinny just right. You look at the timetable – 3 minutes – then back at her. She really is good-looking.

She looks up when she sees the train arriving and you try to look casual yet sexy – sexy? How do you look sexy on a train platform? – in case she looks at you, but she doesn't, she looks straight past you, and you look to the heavens pleading for some luck, even though you know there's no one looking down on you because you don't believe in all of that.

The train arrives, and you dawdle behind as she looks for a seat. You get the one opposite her – lucky – and she's looking out the window with a dreamy look in her eyes. Maybe she's dreaming about meeting someone. Maybe you're just what she's looking for. Then suddenly she notices you looking and looks you straight in the eyes and smiles. You blush and look away, then look back and smile a second too late. Awkward.

She goes back to looking out the window; you must look like an eejit, blushing like a little girl. You look at her reflection in the window now because you don't want to keep looking directly at her in case you look like some sort of a weirdo – Jesus, are you a weirdo? – and you see now up close that she really looks beautiful. You're looking for something to say, some way of breaking the ice, but people don't do that really, do they? It looks good in the movies, maybe, but on a crowded train in Ireland on a Monday evening? You'd look ridiculous.

You look at her through the window as she gets off at her stop – she looks just as good from behind – and see her looking for someone. There's a man there, waiting for her. He's good-looking. She looks happy. Boyfriend. Just your luck.

You sigh and look at them leaving as the train pulls away, root around in your handbag looking for your make-up and wonder to yourself why you're always looking in the wrong places, wonder why you always pick the straight ones.

Lost and found

by Emma Viskic

I'm drinking hot chocolate with my daughters when I find my mother. A café is an unexpected place to come across a miracle, but there she is — just tables away. Almost within reach of her unmet grandchildren.

Something bright fills me and I stand up, heart open. The girls raise their faces towards me like expectant sunflowers.

Look, I go to tell them. Look, there she is: the one who gave you your neat pink fingernails, your heel-digging stubbornness, your voices like larks. But the words lodge in my chest, unspoken. The woman is too young, too short, nothing like my mother at all, really.

"Oh," I say instead. "Don't worry. It's nothing."

Their heads lower to their drinks, I sit down and the world continues; the colours a little muted after the unexpected brightness. Not-Mum stirs sugar into her espresso and takes a sip. What a ridiculous mistake to have made — Mum never drank black coffee. And, anyway, she's been dead for twenty years.

A nightcap with Bukowski

by Morgan Roberts

Glass of bourbon poured, on ice. I pour a little more into an eggcup. I'm sitting on the porch, out back, and the streets are silent. It's a dark and still night, and one by one the lights in the houses around mine have been blown out like candles whilst I've lit cigarettes and poured glasses. It looks like the neighbourhood is asleep; it's safe to let him out now.

"I know that you're there, so don't be sad. I know you're there."

I rest a cigarette on the ashtray and unbutton my shirt. I walk my fingers up my chest, to that old familiar place just below my neck. Pushing my fingers in, the skin separates like a broken seal and I run my finger down the central seam of my chest like a zip. Peeling the skin back, just like my shirt before it, I expose my ribcage and there he is – the bluebird in my heart.

I jab my sternum and it cracks, so I can open my ribs like gates. Reaching a hand inside he timidly sits on my finger. I bring him out and stroke his head with another. I kiss his head and he chirps and tweets. He flies down to the table and sings. Sips his eggcup bourbon. Flying up he does little laps of the room. I light a cigarette and he sings a happy song. I let him out at night. When everyone's asleep.

Bread roles

by Jude Bridge

The greasy actor envies the ridiculously good-looking waiter, slinging the hash in this fast-paced, smelly café. With trembling voice, he stammers,

"Are there any openings here? Dishwasher? Kitchenhand? I can work up to waiter ... I just can't ..." he breaks down, "can't be an actor anymore. You have no idea what it's like. They want me to be ... (sob) ... the next James Bond. Please, you gotta help me."

The waiter silently wipes his third hand on his filthy apron, watching the actor's jaw drop. The grafting operation had been expensive, costing a full day's salary, but was well worth it. Now that he can carry nine plates at once, he has the pick of the A-list greasy spoons. He nonchalantly tidies the condiments on the table, letting his extra fingers do the work. The desperate actor scenario is tediously familiar to the waiter.

Every day at least twenty actors attempt to worm their way into a fulfilling career at this prestigious, smoke and frying-fat infused café. These soft-skinned script regurgitators have no idea what it takes to be a waiter. It's always the same old story. They leave their home town and flock to Hollywood, polished silverware shining in their eyes, expecting to immediately get their big break as a maître d' in a swanky restaurant. Two hundred interviews later, strapped for cash, when they can't even get a position as a busboy at a suburban foodhall, they take the only path left open and approach a Hollywood film studio. Through tears and depression, they feature in action, drama, thriller and sci-fi blockbusters. Some of them sink as low as romantic comedies. Ashamed and unable to share their pitiful lives with family or friends, they become isolated and mentally disturbed. The studios feed on this opportunity and cast them in wacky adventure movies featuring children and animals.

"I'll tell you something for nothing," said the waiter. "Next place you try, put a little more effort into showing your commitment to the hospitality industry."

He consulted his order pad and his eyes darkened.

"You just ordered the Early Bird Special but we stopped serving breakfast at ten-thirty."

Striking a deal

by Diane Simmons

The bedroom floor is messy – clothes, a half-empty rucksack, filthy Converse trainers dangling from the chair. And it stinks of teenage boy. Susan steps over a pile of T-shirts, picks up her son's sweatshirt, smells it, checks to see that she hasn't woken him. It's unlikely – it's only nine in the morning – he should be good for another four hours at least. She has her story ready though in case she disturbs him.

She kneels on the floor and opens a side pocket of Matt's rucksack, then another, then tries the large pouch on the front. She swears when each search reveals nothing more than chewing gum and screwed up tissues. Tipping the rucksack upside down, she shakes the contents on to the floor, rummages, swears again. Her head aches and she feels wound tight like the elastic band on the propeller planes he used to be so obsessed with when he was little. Finding nothing, she reaches for his jeans and feels in the pockets.

"What the fuck?" He is awake, glaring.

"I was just sorting out your washing."

He snorts, sits up. "Yeah, sure, Mother. Sure you are. I told you last night I haven't got anything."

"I don't believe you!"

"Fine. Whatever. Just quit looking through my fucking stuff will you."

She bites her thumbnail, tries not to let him hear the quiver in her voice.

"Do you think I'm stupid – that I don't know what weed smells like?" She puts down his jeans and stares. "You promised me, Matt!"

"Just fuck off, Mum and let me get some sleep," he snaps, lying back down on the bed and closing his eyes. "Shut the door on the way out."

She doesn't leave. She picks up his jacket, and when she finds nothing, reaches for the canvas bag he carries everywhere. As she lifts it off the floor, he is up, out of bed, but she gets to the bag first. The weed isn't even hidden.

"Shit, Matt – you've got loads here!"

He lies back down, sighs. "You can have a teenth – no more. I promised Aiden and his mates."

She smiles, takes the plastic bag. When she is nearly out the door, he shouts to her,

"I want fucking paying this time!"

Perfect word

by Amanda Huggins

Lydia looked out of the hall window at the snow-muffled street and remembered her father's word for the glitter frosting that danced on lamp-lit snow: crackledust. She had never been sure about it. Snow didn't crackle, it crunched.

She stood in the hallway, surrounded by the neatly packed boxes and bin liners containing her father's clothes. She had performed the task of sorting through them accompanied by a bottle of wine, packing systematically and methodically, without pause for the thoughts and memories that would have made it impossible. Jumpers, trousers, belts, shirts, ties; all neatly folded and coiled.

At the bottom of the banister was his green cardigan, the one with a hole in the sleeve and the leather buttons. She was so used to seeing it there that she had overlooked it earlier. Her father had given that a made-up name too: swabbler. The cardigan that he wore for relaxing. For swabbling. Lydia thought it was a lovely word. She wrapped it around her shoulders and opened the front door to greet the silent early-hours world.

The snow was falling faster now. She threw her head back to catch the soft, fat flakes, and they melted like communion wafers on her tongue. She had refused to take communion after the funeral, it would have been a sham, even though it was what her father had believed in. The body of Christ couldn't save her, only the blood of Christ; the wine that she drank to lessen the unexpected weight of her grief.

As she stood in the garden, she realised that although this house would always be her childhood home, soon it would belong to someone else, and she would never visit it again. She would never call her parents' number and hear her father say 'wotcher' with an upper-class accent, or eat a whole plate of her mother's Yorkshire puddings filled with her father's onion gravy. She would never be late for her train because of the dining room clock that was permanently twelve minutes slow.

And now she was going to have to find a new normal, a normal without the certainties of her childhood. And maybe now, at the age of 51, it was time to become a grownup and think of her own word for lamp-lit snow; to come up with something more apt.

It glittered under the streetlights, a million pinprick diamonds, a dusting of crystal kali waiting to pop and fizzle in her mouth. She wrapped her father's cardigan tightly around herself and found that she was brushing away silent tears with the rough wool sleeves.

It was obvious to her now that crackledust was the perfect word for snow-frosting. She didn't need to think of a new one.

Not everything had to change.

The boy

by Eileen Herbert-Goodall

He sat up in bed and stared out the window; there was little else to do in hospital. At least his room was private and offered a decent view. He could see towering buildings and glass walls that glinted in the sun. There were cranes, too; with limbs the colour of hazard orange, they resembled giant metal insects.

The boy stared hard. It was still there, he saw; a nest perched on a ledge of the building opposite, its frame of sticks and leaf litter jammed tight into a concrete corner. In the wind it shivered, threatening to fall down onto the street. The bird that lived there was striking; it was an eagle with a wingspan stretching nearly four feet across, and feathers the colour of a gathering storm, all white and grey. Occasionally, he saw the bird watching him with black eyes that caught the sunlight. His imagination afforded them time alone together, and it was then that he'd let the bird perch on his forearm. They'd be out in fresh air, perhaps in a park filled with pine trees that swayed gently, whispering in the breeze. Stroking the eagle's rounded chest, he'd watch as it tilted its head to inspect him with a beady stare. And in his dreams, he'd often join the bird as it glided about the city, soaring above traffic. At such times, they were both free, beholden to no one.

For now, the bird was nowhere to be seen, but it would return; this he knew from experience. So he waited, scanning the blue sky that stretched forever beyond the hospital's walls.

A nurse entered the room. "Hey, mate. How are you today?"

"Good," he said, without thinking.

"That's the way." She walked forward and picked up the chart that hung on the metal frame of his bed. He'd seen this nurse several times before; she was always friendly. He looked past her, out the window. It was around midday, he figured; the sunshine would be warm.

"Time to check your levels," the nurse said.

Looking at her, the boy nodded.

She rubbed a spot on his forearm with a wet swab. "Are your mum and dad coming up later?"

"I guess."

Furrowing her brow, she prepared the needle with speedy competence. "Another week or so in here and then you'll be home free."

"I hope so," he said.

"I know so." She stepped forward and smiled. "Right then, hold out your arm, love."

The boy did as he was told. Pushing through his skin and into muscle, the needle felt hot and hard, but he didn't blink an eyelid. While the nurse extracted his blood, he looked away and fixed his gaze out the window once more. Immediately, he caught sight of the bird. It came into land with wings fluttering, talons stretched wide, and positioned itself expertly upon the nest. When the eagle turned to look his way, the boy grinned.

Lily's mouse

by Angus Stewart

Lily sat in the garden and sipped her tea. All the alcohol was gone. Lily was a lager girl mostly - one of the lads - but when the craving got really bad, she preferred vodka.

All the other girls were out. They weren't supposed to see these solo drinking sessions, even though some of them already knew. A solo tea session was hardly a criminal act, but still... sitting out alone on a cool evening (as opposed to open, direct sunshine) could easily ring strange and worrying to the more narrow-minded fashion undergraduate. These girls. A couple of them were real Nazis.

The tea was bitter.

The book at Lily's side was dry and splayed in the grass. *The Pearl* by Steinbeck. She didn't want to read, the words and texture made her head sting. And *The Pearl* was deadly boring. Instead she sipped her tea and watched the sky. Its colour was changing.

Something stirred in the weeds. A cat pranced forth, carrying something light. Lily let her sore eyes drift downward. It was a kill. She rose and the cat froze. It eyed her and she took another step. The cat gave her space.

"Hey puss. What've y'got."

Lily's words sounded sad. Not for the kill. She was sure it would be fine.

It wasn't fine. It was a little brown mouse, still except for the whiskers which slowly inhaled, exhaled.

"Hey mouse," said Lily, close to toneless. She crouched to pick it up. "Are you hurt?"

She touched the mouse's hind leg and rolled it over from one palm into the other.

"You're dying, aren't you?"

The cat watched, eyes soft and wide, and it drew a little closer.

"Hey cat," said Lily. "Come look."

The cat and the sad girl watched as the mouse became still. Lily clasped the warm brown body inside her two cupped palms and rose again. The cat peered up to her, still keeping his distance.

Lily walked past him and strolled to the far end of the garden. Her landlord kept a little compost pile between the small trees that grew at his fence-posts, and it was here in the shade she buried the mouse.

"Oh cat," she said, and turned. "This mouse isn't my first."

The cat followed her into the middle of the garden and flopped down into the grass. She coochie-cooed and he drew close. They played and cuddled. Lily forgot about some of the ache in her head, but she still felt slow and heavy. The stars came out.

Her tea was cold.

A few lights flicked on back inside. The girls were home.

The cat padded for the bushes.

"Don't go," said Lily, weak and only half-meaning it. "I need you here. I need you with me."

Sofa boat

by Richard Spalding

My street finally flooded this morning, so I made myself a boat. I taped all the empty shampoo bottles from the floor of the shower together and taped those around the bottom of the sofa. I made a cup of tea, sat back down, and waited.

The water entered quite politely, apologetic but business-like, and carried me slowly out of the living room and down the corridor. I sipped quietly at my tea as water's murky bailiffs escorted me out of the doorway and into the street. Lampposts still nobly lined the pavements, though water paid them no heed, shortening them, patiently eroding their paintwork. Telegraph poles stood amongst them, the masts of great hulking vessels sleeping somewhere beneath the waves.

I bobbed further from my old house. Mrs Green from number 43 floated past in her bathtub, her dog asleep in a saucepan not far behind, his lead tied to one of the taps. The Edwards family waved cheerily from their rooftop as I passed them. Richey shouted something, but the snorkel muffled his voice, so I simply raised my teacup in appreciation and sailed on past.

Cars were listing idly down at the junction, bunched awkwardly together, a small red Micra still indicating right. I continued to glide along past the rows of sudden bungalows, and accepted a hearty refill from Mr. Bradfield, who sailed past semi-submerged in his wheelie bin, waving a kettle in one hand and a milk bottle in the other.

I drifted by the old school house, and watched the boys in their short trousers diving gleefully out of high windows. Teachers floated nearby, grappling with sodden textbooks, wagging wet fingers and offering ineffectual scaldings.

A hamster came past doing backstroke. I took off my shoes and scooped it into the left one, letting it float away again.

I dangled my bare feet in the water as I approached the main road, a vast shipping canal opening out into a sea, an ocean, a watery world. Lanes and lanes of cheery travellers, in buckets, in armchairs, in bathtubs and in cupboards, all washed past me as I headed out, on my sofa, with my tea, happily flooded and wet.

The elephant

by Alex Bruty

An elephant appears in our bedroom. It's huge, wrinkled, apologetic looking. At first, I feel angry we won't be able to continue ignoring our problems; not now the elephant has actually arrived in physical form. But then, as it makes a nervy little coughing noise, I start to feel sorry for it. It must be hard turning up in places it's needed but not wanted - a tiring yet rewarding job.

It leans forward, tries to look smaller. Shame it's not gardening advice we require; it looks like it'd be much more comfortable outside.

You look the other way.

"Someone should say something," I say.

The elephant smiles encouragingly at us both before speaking.

"Please try your best not to be embarrassed; I really have heard it all before. And, obviously, I'm not one to judge - they were very clear about that in the job description."

"What a terrible cliché all of this is," you roll your eyes. "It'll be wanting a bun next."

"That would be terribly nice,' says the elephant. "We might need some tea as well - you two have an awfully large amount to talk about. Let's start with your childhoods."

Coming back to Primorsk

by Anna Nazarova-Evans

This is what we left here in Primorsk, Suburb by the Sea, twenty-eight years ago, following the tank shadows directing us out of the country, like arrows:

Brand new white blocks of flats, freshly painted and decorated; the road leading up to the beach, busy with people wearing cotton shirts and dresses; wise moustached men that sold ripe fruit in more colours that I could name back then, who addressed me as "little girl" and my mother as "beautiful"; the stalls with caramel almonds, homemade lollies, cotton candy and ice cream under blue parasols to stop them melting in the desert sun; white Volgas, bodywork gleaming fresh off the conveyor belt; the fat groomed fishermen cats; and the greatest thing of all – a slice of silver turquoise on the horizon wedged between the blocks of flats and wooden dachas like a piece of pineapple in a Pina colada, smelling of salt and oil and seaweed and all things wonderful, that haunted my dreams for years on, long after we left.

"Don't go back there," they say when we ask for directions, but Mum is already hailing a cab.

The taxi drops us off outside a rickety hut in the midst of cement dust. The dust blanket lays on the road into town, the pavement, the seesaw in the kindergarten. We walk around desolate back streets for a while, until we find the fork in the road from which you used to be able to see the beach.

The blocks of flats, much smaller than I remember them, have turned muddy and black in places. Rust has stained the sea view balconies. There are no trees of any sort. Four men play dominos on a plastic table by the side of the road, smashing the pieces down hard, their clothes old and grey. One of them has tied his goat to the nearest lamppost and the animal chews on the remnants of grass by the pavement. Seagulls make sad screeching noises as they fly into the sun. My mouth tastes like cotton wool and I go into a local shop to get a drink. The lady behind the counter is wrapped into faded shawls and skirts despite the warm weather.

"How come you're here?" she asks taking my manats and handing me the change.

"We used to live here," I say smiling.

"You?" she takes a long, measured look at my clothes. I push my Radley bag behind. She slowly follows me and stands in the doorway.

Mum and I try to make out the colours between the dilapidated shapes by the beach, but all we can see is a tall concrete fence.

"Where's the sea gone?" Mum asks shielding her eyes. We both turn and look at the shop keeper. She chews on something looking towards the horizon and for a minute nothing breaks the silence except for the domino players.

"The sea is for the rich now," she finally says.

A jolly good fellow

by Sharon Telfer

They line us all up in the schoolyard. Me and Billy too, though we've work in the fields with summer come early and everything ripe before it should.

Ma'd scraped Evie's hair into pigtails.

"Stop your fussing, Evangeline Carter," she said. "Don't you want to look pretty for Mr Pritchard's fare thee well?"

Evie just stood shaking her head while Ma tried to fix the ribbons, 'til Ma give her a clip. Last harvest, you could no more hush Evie's prattle than you could stop a lark's beak. She don't say much, though, these days.

All on us, in us Sunday best, holding them little flags from the day they crowned the new King. Vicar says summat, how sad Mr Pritchard is going away so sudden, like. Mr Pritchard, he goes red in the sun while we sing 'For He's a Jolly Good Fellow' and waves us flags and all the grown-ups join in.

Along the line he come, shaking each on us by the hand. Folks is always saying, how he's such a fine schoolmaster, taught us such nice manners. But when he comes to me and Evie, Evie hides behind my legs, like she's shy.

I grip his hand firm, though it's smooth and slippy with sweat. I look at him square, man to man, like. And I say the words real careful, just how I've said each one in my head stooping over the cut corn,

"Godspeed to the city, sir. You will never want to come back to our little village, I am sure."

Sun's in his eyes, maybe, leastways he keeps 'em down, cheeks blazing like poppies.

And Evie slips her fingers into mine, and I squeeze 'em soft back, as Mr Pritchard pulls his hand away and goes off down the line.

Subsidence

by Samantha White

It's six o'clock and the golf club veranda is the coolest place I can find. Beneath the slowly swooshing latticed fans, the tables are sticky with spilt drinks and the fine, black residue that hangs in the air and lightly dusts our houses, our cars, our skin. I slap at another sharp sting behind my knee and feel the blood sticky between my fingers.

At the far end of the veranda, a group of older women huddle around a lazy Susan full of cheese cubes and kabana. One of them is rummaging through her bag for coins to give the bored bartender tasked with selling tickets for the meat raffle. She drops the money into his outstretched hand and says something that makes her friends snigger. I can't hear their words over the screech of the corellas roosting in the trees along the fence line.

A hand lands on my shoulder. It's Peter, an older engineer from my husband's department. When we wives get together to drink over-chilled Chardonnay and buy colourful homewares from the latest party plan, we roll our eyes at Peter and the way he twitches his nose at the end of each sentence. We offer exaggerated commiserations to whichever of us was seated next to him at the last dinner. We mimic his monotone and laugh at the handkerchief he keeps in his pocket. I don't tell them he reminds me of my dad.

"Andy was still underground when I left," says Peter, "So he won't be back for dinner. You'll still join us, though?"

I nod. It's what we do every Friday. The men come home and scrub the coal from under their nails, inside their elbows, along their jaws. We wives stand in our standard-issue bathrooms and apply make-up that will slide off our faces within an hour. Then we meet at the golf club, its rickety veranda looking out over scrubby greens and our cookie-cutter company houses.

At dinner, Peter is telling me about his uni days, about the time he did a delivery job for a bloke he'd met down the pub.

"So there I am," he says, "a bunch of dodgy meat in the back of this unrefrigerated truck, no heavy vehicle licence, six hundred k's from where I'm supposed to be, and a hitchhiker who says he's a Dutch aristocrat".

I throw my head back and laugh and for the first time in months I can breathe. But then I see Karina smirking at me across the table, so I roll my eyes and grimace. When I realise that Peter has seen, my eyes sting and I can't finish my chicken. He doesn't tell me the rest of the story. We sit silently, my thumbnail scoring crosses over the itchy welts dotting my legs.

This is the last time I will see Peter. Over the weekend, the aneurysm will rupture and he will die alone on his kitchen floor - mottled-grey linoleum, wood-grained, identical to my own.

Swifts

by Jude Higgins

She should have offered Matthew, the plumber, a cup of tea, but instead she used a sharp voice and told him he had to be out of the house by midday. A solid young man with a round pleasant face, he appeared unfazed by her tone.

"We'll have to see," he said. "Depends on what I find up there."

That made her panic. Earlier, when she'd flushed the toilet, everything had floated to the surface and had threatened to flood the bathroom. The water, with its contents, had subsided eventually, but there still might be traces. Matthew didn't look squeamish. Perhaps plumbers were like nurses, able to copy with bodily emissions.

In the garden, she sat in a deck chair on the overgrown lawn and looked at her feet. A red painted toenail emerged through a hole in her tights, like a reminder of her youth. It was funny how some parts of the ageing body stayed young, while others sagged and wrinkled. Her feet and legs were the most youthful part of her. They used to be admired and not that long ago.

Matthew came out and looked mildly at her. He held a thermos and poured himself a tea.

"You need a new siphon," he said. "I'll have to go and get one, then disconnect the pipes." He tipped three packets of sugar into his cup and spent some time stirring it in. "I'm likely to be here most of the day."

"Out of the question," she said. But it was hard to make her voice authoritative.

"It's how it is," he said and stared up at the swifts zipping across the sky.

She wondered whether to say anything further, like *My daughter's coming with the little ones. We can't do without the toilet.* Or. *I've got an urgent appointment with my lawyer.* None of that was true. She had no children, no appointments with lawyers anymore and no-one to see. She could have said. *I was trying a different version of myself. I've been too nice, too compliant. That's why I'm here in the garden with a hole in my tights. That's why I can't flush everything away.*

She looked down at her big toe. The varnish had nearly all flaked off, her nail needed cutting. Whatever must she look like in her scruffy fleece, her hair all over the place?

But Matthew hadn't noticed. He leaned against the patio doors and drank his tea, his eyes still following the swifts.

"They'll be on their way soon," he said, watching them line up on the telegraph wire. "But they'll be back again next year. At least that's certain." He drained his cup and screwed it back on the thermos. "Don't worry. We'll sort you out today, no problem."

He sounded very sure.

Where the plan first occurred to her

by Amy J Kirkwood

She'd noticed the ghost-house on the horizon, where the mountains turned from green to a hazy, distant blue. Now, the surrounding grass ripples like water in the breeze, brushing her ankles so lightly it could be a mistake.

But it's not. Sophie is *supposed* to be here. She feels it as the drizzle ebbs and flows around her, her feet making shadow-marks in the damp earth.

Her brother isn't so sure. "Can we go back? *Please*?"

"No. I'm s'posed to be looking after you. Mum'll get cross."

"I'm not allowed to walk more than half an hour – the doctor said." Joe's voice has that familiar whiny, wheezy quality.

Her younger brother's resistance makes her angry, because this is her destiny – to find a ghost in this abandoned house – and yet again Joe is ruining it, just like he does when he takes up all of Mum's time with his *problems*.

"Shut up. It'll be fun."

Sophie takes his hand as a pre-emptive apology – Joe won't think it's fun and she knows it. Also, if she leads like this he will follow, because he loves her.

The house stands three storeys tall; only, the middle storey is missing, gutted like a mackerel skeleton where the flesh has rotted away. Dad used to take them mackerel fishing before it was bad for Joe's heart. She and Dad went alone after that twice, until Mum said Joe felt left out. By the time next summer came, her father was gone – tired of waiting for Joe's transplant.

Sophie is tired, too.

Joe allows himself to be led through the crumbling wooden door.

Inside, shadows twist, cloaking the walls with a thin grey film. They climb the stone steps to the missing middle storey, Sophie's breaths light and Joe's heavy.

Hand in hand, they stand on a ledge at the top of the stairs, backs to the wall. Sophie teeters slightly as she cranes her neck forward to check for phantoms. A rotten rope ladder hangs from the roof – a way up, to the top floor – but it's too dangerous.

No ghosts. Her heart folds in on itself – again, disappointment.

"I'm not going up that ladder. I'm not *allowed*." Joe's voice cuts the silence.

Sophie looks at Joe and tilts her head. What if she got it wrong? What if her destiny wasn't to find a ghost, but to give the house a ghost of its very own? Joe's pathetic frankfurter lips wobble. Frankfurters were Dad's favourite.

"I'd think you were *so* brave if you climbed it," Sophie says.

"Really?"

He'll do it – of course he will.

She considers.

She raises an arm – ready to help him up.

But then she looks into his eyes: murky green, just like hers, and Dad's. Mum's are blue.

"No. Don't be *stupid*." She huffs, trying not to notice his wheezes as they descend the steps – away from the ghost-house, back onto the earthy path.

No ghosts today.

I am in the wool

by Sarah Baxter

My hands take up rosewood pins; they are witch's sticks. The wood warms, my knuckles swell and fingers thin. My addiction is merino or cashmere, cut with silk. Pure alpaca's pricey but washes well. I loathe acrylic, which feels like squeaky cheese.

I am in the wool.

The knit stitch is masculine. He thrusts upward from right to left, tugs and hooks the yarn. The purl is feminine. She slides under to lift up and complete the wale. She's worn on the reverse, against the skin and hardly seen.

The rows advance, locked in opposition.

A half-finished sleeve cries, until it's picked up and soothed from the wicker basket. I make sweaters and cardies, wristlets and shawls. They deepen like snow drifts in my bottom drawer.

I observe a blonde hair, snared in the weave of a raven-coloured scarf.

I am in the wool.

He prefers clothes made from synthetic fibre, shipped from eastern factories by the tonne. He wears esters and amides, which smoulder contemptuously when dried on the electric heater.

He cannot stand the touch of wool against his neck. He swears it enrages his eczema and compels me to wash my lanolin-scented hands before I am permitted to caress his face. At the market, I buy pink four-ply for booties. The twenty-five gram balls, each bound with paper strips, gleam. But their mirror form within me, moulded by my woman's craft, unravels in A&E while he's out of town.   ! I take a taxi home and unpick my trifling, pastel reverie. I hold vigil as the muss burns, atop a pyre of pine cones in the hearth.

I do not tell him of our charm that I'd cast off.

One night, as he slumbers. I inspect a ball of fluff gathered in his yawning navel. I take it as a sign.

The next night I reach for the crochet hook, secreted under my pillow. I hike out the fuzz, a tumbleweed of belly hair and goodness knows what else. And there it is -- the knot created when his umbilicus was snipped. I plunge the hook into the centre of its tight folds and pull.

I pluck and pluck.

As dawn breaks, he is now one hundred-odd kilos of second-hand yarn, still crimped from his original stitches.

I wind him into a myriad of balls of different shades and knit a perfect square to test the tension. I read the neat, relaxed stitches as if they spell the words in my burgeoning heart. I calculate the number of rows needed for an arm, a thigh, a trunk, a mouth with an unfamiliar kiss.

I bring out the double-pointed needles, the ones my mother gave me, and cast on.

Cup of tea

by Ursula Dewey

Was I an inconsequence? A result of no import? Data sewn onto a graph with too weak a thread? An anomaly to dismiss?

The question hangs in the silence. The noose of it tightening and lifting me off the ground. My feet stumble before I can speak. Your mouth opens before I can ask a thing. You fill the air with observations about the weather. The glisten of the sunlight on frosted branches, like fairy dust you say. Like magic.

"Isn't it cold?"

Was I the fruit of inconvenience then? Perhaps that was it? A burden to yield. Let it be. And be. The pear swells and ripens from the tree and falls. Where it lies and leathers. Puckered edges. Insides turning to rot. Here I am, your daughter. Decades later. Over ripe.

You had your reasons. You were young. Unmarried. And he was. You place a withered hand on mine. Funny how history repeats.

I can't quite stand the thought of it. And yet here we are, reunited. A café in Askrigg. The cushion of the Yorkshire Dales rolling far and wide around us like padding.

You had started to visit me in my sleep. The permeations of how you will be, of how this meeting will go. I woke this morning with a sudden feeling of dread. We've pushed ourselves apart for so long, coped so well without the other, that all that there can be left to explore is emptiness.

You smile out the window, not able to look at me. Your eyes rest upon my reflection in the glass. The transparent version, through which you can still see the snow, the trees, the stone houses, topped with white, undisturbed.

"Pot of tea alright?" I ask.

"Oh yes please. Never did care for coffee." You say.

We sit in silence a moment more, until the tea arrives and we both pour and add a dash of milk, watching it run shapes through the water and transform.

Sign, signifier, signified

Or, the deconstruction of the end of an evening

by Ingrid Jendrzejewski

"Love you," I mumble, turning off the bedside light.

"What do you mean by that?" you say in the resulting darkness, and I can tell from your voice you're nowhere near ready for sleep.

I try to answer by pulling the covers up over my ears, but you just say 'Hey,' and repeat your question.

"I mean the same thing I mean every night," I say.

"A signified concept can vary between contexts," you say, your voice low, as if you're trying to sneak in the last word.

"Well," I say, "in this particular context, what I meant by 'love you' was 'Goodnight. Sleep well. And I care about you.'"

"And also," you say, "You meant, 'I'm tired, I want to sleep, don't start anything.'"

"I did not."

"Yes you did."

"I did not. Don't I get any say in what I mean?" I ask.

"The author is dead and all that," you say, and I can't tell if you're being flippant or peevish, so I turn the light back on and look you in the eye.

"Yes, but you're not reading a text. You're talking. To me. And I'm here to help you revise your assumptions about what it is I mean when I say 'love you'."

You make that noise you make which causes me to put my annoyed face on.

"Seriously," I say. "Can't it be a nice thing? A nice way to end the evening? Can't we just agree to make it an affectionate utterance? Locate meaning between the two of us?"

"Do you want to have sex?" you ask, and, for the life of me, I can't read your expression.

I pause, then sigh. "Okay, so maybe I did mean 'don't start anything'."

Your smugness creeps through the air like a smell.

"But," I say, "words have a surplus, a web, a whole field of meaning. It's not fair to pin 'love you' down to just one thing. Can't we just be happy with a multiplicity of meanings? Let those signifiers slide?"

"Sounds kinky," you say.

"What, you actually want to have sex? Really?"

For a moment, I think I see your jaw tense. "Not really," you say.

"So then what exactly are *you* trying to say?" I ask. I lift an eyebrow and the silence between us says a bit too much.

"Nothing," you say. "Or everything."

Caught unawares by the inherent instability of language and meaning, we sit in bed blinking at each other, looking for a sign. You squeeze my hand, but neither of us know what it means.

"Love you," you say, and I repeat what have become your words.

After a moment, you turn out the light, but it's a long time before we close our eyes.

The cliff

by Rebecca McPhearson

I paused to catch my breath; fingers hooked into the volcanic rock face. The wind carried strings of mist like cobweb over the stone. Every muscle in my body ached and yet the tension in my limbs remained, trembling on the edge of control. The cliff loomed above, a cruel overhang, sharp black against the pale fog. Below me lay only the shroud of darkness.

I knew that I had picked a foolish route to climb, yet a stubborn anger refused to let me alter my course. I had been careless too, dashing my hands on outcrops as jagged as shattered glass. Although I tore my clothes to provide makeshift padding and bandage, blood still trickled down my forearms, congealing in the grime and sweat. For as long as I could remember I had defied gravity, propelled upward by the dream of the summit, until a simple realization stopped me. There was no summit. I cried then, ice in my lashes. What difference could it make if I fell now? Why struggle upward against the ache, against the pain, against the relentless rock, when in the end, I knew I must fall? I looked down. The mist that swirled in the darkness below offered only oblivion. I could let go. I could tuck my hands into the warmth of my armpits and fall back into open air. I could almost feel the release. I jolted in panic, my hands gripping tight, my stomach in my throat. For a moment I closed my eyes and concentrated on breathing. Fear held me to the rock. The terror of the drop overcame any rational motivation. I looked up. The cliff offered nothing. No threat, no taunt, no encouragement. How long could I cling like moss on the stone before my grip failed me? Just then, a little shard of blue caught my eye, bobbing in the wind above the lip of the overhang. Through the mist I could make out a tiny, ice blue flower, bowed by the wind. The scrap of colour provided a landmark if nothing more.

I pried a stiff hand from the rock, fingers feeling for a higher hold. I hooked in and took the weight, straining the tendons in my arm, stabbing knives into my shoulder, releasing my legs to find a new foothold. I would climb at least as far as that flower.

Emily's elephant

by Helen Anderson

Emily's diary is pale pink, with a blank, black spine. It does not draw attention to itself in the row of exercise books and laminated set texts. She does not hide it under her mattress, because that is the first place they would look. They are starting to think that they should have a little look.

Dad thinks that they should turn the whole room upside down and that the end justifies the means. Mum favours a subtle rifle through her drawers, being careful to put the mess back into its exact position. She doesn't feel comfortable with it. They decide to seize their chance, the next time Emily sneaks out with him. She never brings him back here. They heard rumours that he has his own bedsit, on the other side of the railway line, like a bad 80's song.

They wait for her to go out, but she starts stopping in. Mostly, she's hunched over her books. Mum thinks that the penny has finally dropped about studying but Dad points out the nosedive in her mock exam marks. One time, Emily spends a long time in the bath, and they almost go for it. Dad stands guard on the landing and Mum psyches herself up at the bedroom door.

They lose their nerve, at the last minute, when it comes down to it. They both pretend that they think they hear her pulling the plug out, and they abort their mission. The diary stays on the desk, between Emily's revision timetable and her lucky mascot.

While they debate the morality of snooping – of giving trust and letting go – Emily slowly turns sixteen. The diary swells. One day, quite soon, it will burst open and scatter its contents throughout the house and there will be no ignoring it.

Pocket wishes for scraps of paper

by John Heggelund

School but every time the bell rings someone kisses you.
Sports but you can participate even if you're bad.
SATs but no one asks you about your score.
Parents but they love you more no matter what.
Guns but instead of killing they garishly display inadequacies.
Me but I don't act so scared all the time.
Cell phones but they talk so you always have a friend.
Sleep but you never wake up only dream deeper and deeper.
Breathing but you don't need air it's just to feel alive.
Fingertips but they aren't where you end only the beginning.
Me but I meet people and never feel weird about asking for their
    number.
Parties but there's always a quiet boy who's just shy not weird.
Getting wasted but you don't make bad decisions you only have more
    fun.
Sex but it doesn't matter if the other person is beautiful or not.
Friends but they never make jokes about you they always make you
    feel better about yourself.
Karma but it demands to be heard.
Weed but it doesn't stink or make your eyes red.
Family but you don't have to hide anything because they understand
    or want to.
College but instead of grade points you collect job vouchers like Kool-
    Aid coupons.
Boyfriends but they don't care when you feel dumb and speechless no
    matter what happens or anyone says or does.
Apartments but they don't stink when you don't clean them.
Clothes but they make you look good and want to go out.
Wine but it only makes you happy.
TV but there's actually something good on to watch.
Me but I don't drink alone or talk to the phone like it responds.
Delivery drivers but they don't call you shut-in bitch for not tipping
    when they refuse to come up.

Men but they treat women like we could do something if it came down
    to it.
Me but at least I go out to the bar.
Me but I can smoke enough weed to float away.
Me but this can't possibly be what I'm supposed to be doing.
Me but I can explain myself and how I feel and what the hell is going
    on.
Me but I'm ready to change I just don't know how.
Me but there's no more buts I just do it.
Me but I'm not the only thing holding me back.
Me but I act like I want to get better.
Me but I sound like I give a shit.
Me but me,
But me,
But me,
But me,
But me,
But me.

Small mercies

by Karen Jones

When you play Monopoly with your brothers, let them win, she says. Boys don't like to lose, especially not to girls. She's patting her face with a powder pad, as though her features will fall off if they're not pressed in place. When she's out at a dance, I sneak into her room and play at being her, being beautiful, being good with make-up. When a boy asks you out, always say yes. It doesn't matter if he's not the best looking, the cleverest, the funniest – it takes a lot of courage for a boy to ask a girl out, so be grateful and always, always say yes to boys. I take her lipstick and pout as I smear the scarlet grease over my too-thin lips on my too-fat face with its barely-there eyes. I can never look like her, but I can do as I'm told. And so, I did. I said yes to boys. All the boys. The ugly boys, the short boys, the boys who smell like sewers and the boys with urgency mapped out in spots on their red faces. When your brothers get up in the morning, draw their curtains, make their beds – be useful. The liquid eyeliner almost makes me have eyes. Not eyes like hers – not violet, not startling, but at least existing. My mother made me easy – a thing she never was to me. I'm sure it wasn't her intention, but I was nothing if not obedient, so I said yes over and over again. Until I finally got it, finally realised what I'd become. I used her cold cream to erase the face I'd painted. Then I said no. I said no over and over again. But the boys told me they'd heard about me and no really meant yes, and did what they wanted anyway. That hurt more, so I went back to being the girl my mother made me – the yes-girl, the old-before-her-years girl, the never-as-pretty-as-her-mother-so-beggars-can't-be-choosers girl. Now she complains that I never gave her grandchildren. Oh, but I did, Mother Dear. So many half-formed girls that neither of us got to hold or mould. Small mercies, Mother. Be grateful.

Messenger

by Brian Wilson

I send my brother a message asking whether he's seen the latest Aronofsky film. I send my sister a message asking when she's back from Enniskillen. I send my three best friends three generic messages: what's new on Netflix, an article about Game of Thrones, a meme involving Tom Hardy's Batman character, Bane.

With each message her name sinks a little bit lower, but I can still see it when I launch messenger, so I send a few more. I send an old work colleague a message saying *what's up it's been a while.* I send a current work colleague a message saying *hi do you happen to have the shift supervisor's number?*

I'm in the middle of sending my cousin a YouTube video when the phone vibrates in my hands. It's from her.

hey

I am careful not to open it. I resume sending messages. I send my brother a message asking whether he's seen the latest Villeneuve film. I meant Denis Villeneuve.

Captivity

by Jennifer Riddalls

Ahead of me, Rex's black leathery nose is suctioned to the ground, inhaling everything that has come before us. I wonder if there's been anyone else here, besides us, since yesterday ...or even the day before. We are like zoo animals, each foot landing exactly in our own footprints, wearing down the earth, pacing in the cage. Distressed. Something unfamiliar in my peripheral makes me stop so suddenly that Rex doesn't notice at first, continuing forward 'til his lead strains against my hand. There on the chain-link padlocked gate someone has hung a little plastic tiger, its back legs hooked through the wire as if part way through escaping.

James loved plastic animals. There are hundreds of animals like these, back in his room, plastic shapes filling plastic tubs. This tiger is filthy, but too bright, too orange. Only something that looked thirty years weathered, all those seasons buzzing around it as the earth spun, would make hope bubble up. Like the time I'd seen the faded, sodden navy cuff of a small glove poking out of the undergrowth. James was wearing plain navy mittens when he disappeared. The promise of information had sent my heart beating frantically. Wanting to know, not wanting to know. I'd dragged it out and was crushed to discover it had five knitted fingers.

I stretch a fingertip towards the tiger; brush a crumb of wet dirt off. The former white of his lower jaw is stained a sludgy brown that will never come clean, never recover. I realise it's been buried, it's too dirty for anything else. Lost under mud, the colour protected... except the tip of one tiger ear is pink where the orange has been sucked out by the sun. My stomach flips and hope simmers. I look past the toy, my eyes pushing it out of focus, to the water treatment plant beyond. The earth around the pumps has been disturbed. Workers must have dug up this forgotten treasure and hung it here for a small podgy hand to reach up and retrieve it.

Rex whines, impatient to complete our routine, and it snaps me into action. I get one of the little bags I use to clean up after Rex and cover my trembling hand with it, awkwardly enveloping it round the tiger, enclosing it in my pocket. I half-drag Rex home in a lumbering jog, his black eyes darting up at me. I abandon him in the hallway, lead trailing and I'm straight upstairs, muddy boots on faded carpet. I stop at the doorway to James' room and remove them. Tipping all the plastic animals onto the floor it only takes a few seconds to spot a near-identical tiger, not muddy, conserved here. A sob escapes me and I'm not sure if its sorrow or relief. Rain starts drumming on the skylight. I close my eyes and pretend the pitter-patter of water is small feet, running towards me.

Sea change

by Sharon Telfer

My heart sank.

I watched it go. It fought hard to keep afloat. I took my boathook, knocked back its jellyfish pulses. I had to make sure. Cracked, it bubbled silver as it dropped, an aspirin fizz then one toxic gulp like mercury breaking from a thermometer. It stopped struggling after that, twisted, turned in the tug of the tide, spiralling slowly down into the deep dark.

I watched until I could see it no more.

My mother warned me. You never know when you might want it back. To shut her up, I marked it by the harbour buoy. I knew I wouldn't need it again. I crossed off years well enough without it, working, eating, sleeping, the sea going out, coming in. Except on stormy nights. The wild clamour of the buoy bell woke me then. I'd hug the pillow over my ears and curse my mother.

But she was right. Of course.

There you were, one day, end of the pier, leaning into the wind like a figurehead. For the first time since I drowned my heart, I licked my roughened, seaside lips and tasted salt.

That night I rowed out and let down my net. I threw back the crabs and the mackerel, rubbed off the barnacle crust by the light of the moon. My pearlescent heart shone, strange, hard, beautiful.

I bent my back to the oars and headed for land, heart thumping like a fresh caught fish.

Pedometry

by Shannon Savvas

Alicia counts her steps. Too many. Too even. Fourteen. The four is wrong, wrong, wrong. She goes back. Starts again. Front door to car door. Fifteen this time. Relief. Even numbers are unlucky. She had bled out Eve at four months, when she was twenty-two. Two and two. Two years later, Paul, again at four, when she was twenty-four.

On the drive to the hospital, she makes herself slow down because the numbers keep distracting her. She counts everything to get there – cars, colours, traffic lights, times between lights, bikes, dogs, pregnant women. She averts her face whenever she passes a CCTV camera. Cameras know. Cameras report. They follow her everywhere. She had noticed the cameras on her previous visits. She is wise to them now. It was after the scans, that she lost her babies. They had looked at the tiny bodies and found them, or her, wanting. They are watching to see if she made a mistake again. She will not allow any more scans. If she did, they would punish her as they did with Eve and Paul.

She has to drive around the hospital block twice until she has counted a fifth pregnant woman. It has to be five or she would lose her baby. Again. This was the first of the dangerous months. The one she couldn't avoid. The fourth.

A sharp right turn prevents her red Honda Civic being sandwiched by two red cars. Cars honk and drivers curse. They don't know. She does. Red. The colour of blood. She hates red. Red is bad, bad, bad.

The carpark attendant indicates a bay by the entrance to the clinic, but it is too exposed. She has to be under the trees for protection, hidden from the eyes on the third floor, which she is sure, knows, are watching her. She has seen the shuttered eyes perch and sweep. Under a shady oak, she parks and click-locks the car. With a deep breath, she checks her watch. She has five minutes and one hundred and thirty-nine steps to get to the antenatal clinic doors. No time to get it wrong. She sets off, counting, counting, counting.

Jenny & I go to Bristol Zoo

by Anthony Dandy

I walk into the Airmen's Mess. Jenny is alone at her breakfast table, waiting for me. Only a few diners – it is early – it is Saturday. She watches as I enter the Mess.

"Hi, I thought you weren't coming."

"Of course I am," I say, a frisson of irritation rippling through me. I have a reputation amongst the airwomen of the station – I never stick to a relationship, too flighty.

I collect my breakfast from the hotplate and join Jenny at her table.

"I have got us a packed lunch," she says, kind eyes. She is a slim pretty airwoman, aged 20. I am a tall slim soldier, aged 19 – been dating a while.

"I am so looking forward to today," I reassure Jenny.

A taxi-ride to Chippenham Station, train to Bristol, taxi to the zoo. It is a warm sunny day; we look at all the animals. We sit on the grass; Jenny unpacks our lunches.

"There you go, James," she says, eager to please, "cheese and tomato, or you can have mine, egg and cress."

We halve them, content in our compromise; so intimate. We drink cider. We fall asleep on the grass, near the flowers.

We awaken together, surrounded by people and picnics.

"I always look like this when I wake up," Jenny says. She looks at me, self-conscious.

"You always look great," I say.

She takes my photo, by the Great Apes.

"Let me take your picture, Jenny." I say.

"I hate having my picture taken," she says.

I don't want to make her uncomfortable, I hold her by the hand and we walk on.

***

We take the evening train back to Chippenham, a meal in a Chinese restaurant, a taxi back to camp. We kiss on the doorstep of the WRAF

Block.

"Thank you for a lovely day."

"Come for me tomorrow, after work, James," Jenny calls after me, as I walk to my block. I wince at her unwitting reminder of my flightiness.

Two months later I am posted to Northern Ireland. We lose touch – my fault. I hear Jenny was posted to Gibraltar.

***

We meet again. She is 59, happily re-married, no longer slim, kind eyes. I am 58, happily married, no longer slim. Jenny shows me the photograph of me, by the Great Apes.

We gaze at the photograph in her hand, together silent. My hand brushes against hers, she takes holds of it. She squeezes my hand gently. For a few moments, I sense how we used to be.

"We had a great day at Bristol Zoo," she says, breaking the silence, releasing her hand from mine.

"We will always have Bristol Zoo," I reply.

I brought her flowers and we talk for hours. Not enough time to say everything. We say goodbye, smiling, happy-sad.

As I leave, I damn my old flighty self; I am glad Jenny is happy. I wish I could make amends with them all...

Drown

by Melissa Goode

Your apartment is like a ship, the Mediterranean below us and as far as we can see. The water is the deepest blue.

    "Makes you want to jump in, doesn't it?" I say.

    "If you did, you'd break every bone in your body."

    I want to say—*you weren't always like this, were you*?

    I sip soda water. You drink orange juice. This is us on the other side of the world to where we started.

***

Six years ago, you picked a magnolia from our neighbour's yard and put it in my hair.

***

I touch the window and feel the wind on the other side, buffeting against it, pushing and pushing.

***

We walk to a pizzeria a couple of blocks from your apartment. You tell me it is the best pizza in Genoa.

    "Let's go back to yours," I say. "Get home delivery."

    "What? No one home delivers here, unless they're rubbish."

    Past your shoulder is the sea, wind-churned, glittering. *When the fuck did we ever care about food, except that we had some, any?*

***

At dinner, you say so little. You order in Italian for us, sounding like you have always lived here. You order two bottles of sparkling water.

    "Are you trying to drown me?" I say.

    My hair and my dress smell of wood smoke.

110

***

Our dog, Boo, died two months ago. I planned to tell you in person, but I cannot say the words—*Boo* or *dog* or *died*.

***

Roy Orbison and K.D. Lang sing "Crying". You smile at me.

***

We walk back to my hotel. You say, for a *nightcap*.

"You don't really say *nightcap*, do you?"

You laugh and your white shirt takes the colours of the sky—orange, purple, pink.

***

You sit on the end of the bed and cover your face with your hands. I dock my phone — Orbison and Lang sing here too. I sit beside you, touch your back. Your skin is hot through the cotton. It burns.

In the minibar you find two whiskey miniatures and say, "I'm surprised these are still here."

You pour two tumblers and top them with a small measure of water. You hand me a glass and I chink it against yours—*saluti*.

"This is more like it," I say.

"You're such a romantic."

"Isn't this more fun than porcini, bocconcini, whatever?"

"Not so far."

You sit beside me on the bed. The whiskey sets my mouth on fire and it tears down my throat and through my limbs.

***

When you tip your head back to drain the glass, I feel the movement as if I am holding your head in my hands. It is one of the ways I miss you, when I am seven hours behind you. Tipping your head back, drinking every last drop.

You take my empty glass and draw the drapes against the last light. You stay where you are, by the window. We remove our clothes.

The miracle man - 1978

by T.E. Condon

He came with a statue, a virgin on a plastic throne - the Miracle Man - whose toy was rumoured to heal even the hopeless cases like you. We knelt around your bed, as the others lit candles to exalt your sickroom into something else.

I hunched near your pillow, my knees in shorts, yours flattened by the quilt. Our little brother slicked pink lipstick onto your lips, and you smiled doll-like as the room hushed.

The Miracle Man whispered his disclaimer - *there are no guarantees* - as he took in your improbable frame, your waxen skin.

The statue was placed on the dresser. Her cold stone stare fixed onto your warm, damp eyes. The Miracle Man announced he would lead the prayers.

He began to recite and we, who had grown used to the extraordinary - the pills, the drips, your concave chest -were now surprised. For some strange affectation was transforming his otherwise even voice into a high-pitched cartoon of a moan.

"Heal herrrrrrrr."

Consonants curved and vowels stretched over your head, your synthetic curls. But the sound was strange and familiar – it was a Movie Star voice.

"The ower of ahr dee-ath!"

Higher, higher, higher, his Hollywood passion filled the room. Twangier, louder, as LA, Alabama and New York all merged into one for your Irish salvation.

We swopped glances. You raised a hairless eyebrow.

He finished Round One on an Amen squeak.

The Rosary beads were set to pause as we waited.

"Lawdy, Lawrdy, Lawrd."

Something was coming, and our brother delivered it. He stared at the man and gasped. *What's up, Doc.* "He sounds like Bugs Bunny!" he declared with true admiration, before being shoved swiftly from the room.

Your shoulders shook first. They trembled with each Bunny keen, as around you we battled against this long-forgotten infection of mirth. The devout fought to stay solemn and failed. A candle was extinguished by a splutter of joy.

The Miracle Man was oblivious as the tears slid down our cheeks, though it was not from cruelty we giggled – for that visitor we had respect – but some new relief.

At last our father stood up and interrupting the man mid-wail, he took him to the hall where the Miracle Man resumed his soft, grave tone.

In the room, your smile stayed wide. The statue was impassive, unimpressed.

We buried you with laughter.

Moby Dick and the beginning of the end

by Ingrid Jendrzejewski

He says Melville was stupid because he constantly refers to Moby Dick as a fish. Moby Dick is not a fish. Moby Dick is a whale. Everyone knows that whales aren't fish and fish aren't whales. Ergo, Melville is not worth reading.

She tries everything she can think of. She discusses poetic language. She suggests that it is Ishmael, not Melville who calls the whale a fish. She asserts that even if Moby-Dick does contain an inherent factual inaccuracy regarding fish and whales, there are many reasons that it is still worth reading. Eventually, when she is tired of arguing, she asks why a whale can't be a fish and why a fish can't be a whale in the context of a novel: a novel is a work of fiction, after all.

None of it works; he is not convinced. Time is passing and it is getting late. He can't get past the whale/fish issue and she can't get past the fact that he can't get past it. He accuses her of being out to sea; she retaliates that it is he who is missing the boat. For better or for worse, they are, on this occasion, able to come up with enough nautical puns to hold off the inevitable sinking that is quietly being prepared for them by the roiling sea.

Egg

by Julia Anderson

"Get lost! Beat it!" I often want to scream at Egg, like the times I shouted at those bullies in junior school thirty years ago for picking on my little sister Mally. Lately, I've been wishing I could leave Egg shaking on the street corner just as I left that pair of skinheads trembling there twenty-five years ago after they'd pushed Mally off her pink-framed bicycle.

"Oi! Leave her alone!" I'd bellowed as I pedalled hard up the road to reach a sobbing Mally. "Our dad ain't gonna be happy about you hurting my sister or damaging her bike," I'd yelled as I skidded to a halt.

The Crombie coated skinhead stopped sneering when it hit him who we were.

"Shit! It's Denny Cable's daughters."

The second skinhead, who had the words Bovver and Skins tattooed on each side of his neck, pleaded,

"Don't tell your old man about us." He dug into the pockets of his blue-and-green tonic trousers and took out two handfuls of loose change. He shoved the shiny new decimal coins mixed in with several grubby thrupennies towards Mally.

Everyone was scared of our dad with his bare-knuckle boxer's frame towering over the town.

Sometimes I wish that Egg had appeared during our childhood because Dad was fighting fit and alive then. He'd have made Egg go away for sure because everyone scarpered when even just his words flew. But Mally only found out about Egg six months ago.

"It's the size of a chicken's egg," she'd sobbed, telling me about her brain tumour. I held both her and my tears.

"We'll get through this together," I told her.

Silence shrouds us in the neurosurgeon's office as Doctor Sullivan studies Mally's scans in the adjacent side-room. Echoes from my school days swirl inside my head. A voice from long ago, my own childhood voice, yearns to escape and yell,

"Hey, Doc! I'll bloody your nose if you hurt my sister."

Of course, I don't shout this out loud; the words remain clogged in my throat along with many other unspoken conversations.

Finally, the neurosurgeon calls us in.

"Please look at your first scan. Can you see the growth?" he says, pointing to an illuminated white mass the exact size and shape of a chicken egg. Mally and I nod; we see Egg.

"Now look at the image taken three days ago." Doctor Sullivan clips the most recent scan up onto the lightbox. We look.

"The tumour's now hummingbird egg size," he says.

Memories stir from deep within me. I'm back in the schoolroom. I smell the chalk dust and I hear the rhythmic sound of Miss Duncan's footsteps on the wooden floor as she walks up and down and in between the rows of desks where we sit in alphabetical order waiting for our Nature Studies lesson to begin. Finally, the teacher stops pacing and starts the lesson.

"Hummingbirds," she says, "lay the smallest bird eggs in the world."

Your own children

by Amanda Huggins

Every August I see my summer boy on the beach. I have watched him grow up from my window. Sometimes I make sketches of him. A boy in Rory's image; caramel-skinned and lathe-thin, like a shaft of sunlight.

I saw him today, crouched over a rock pool, slender fingers entwined with the red tentacles of anemones. His bucket was full of iridescent shells and colourful pebbles that would fade to pale as they dried.

I always wished the summer boy was Rory. I wanted to walk down to Balducci's with him for ice cream sodas, and then varnish the pebbles for him so that they stayed forever bright.

Before he was anything else, Rory was your reassurance that you wouldn't let me down, that you'd finally tell your wife. He was wrapped in the shopping bag with my new skintight jeans, the ones I bought on the day we did the test, the ones I felt so good in. He was in my nervous laugh when I threw the bag across the bed and you pointed out that I may soon be too big for them.

At that moment Rory became my future, in a stuffy room filled with bottles and baby grows. Just the two of us, and you, visiting when you could. And in that future, it was always winter and rough seas.

Then Rory was my forehead against the cool bathroom tiles, and the knot in my stomach whilst I waited for the line to turn blue. And, just like that, he was gone. Gone without touching the sides. Rory wasn't a blue line on a pregnancy test. He was a line missing. He was your obvious relief, your pale smile, your cold fingers on my arm. He was your voice telling me how you would have always been torn between this new baby and your own children. An odd thing to say: your own children. As though Rory would have been less yours in some way.

As I lay awake that night, my relief changed to grief. I mourned the loss of you and I, and the child that I hadn't wanted, but who was already formed in my mind.

In the morning we woke to an altered state, an imperceptible shift, and our words tiptoed around our feelings. The re-appraisal of an affair that had almost become something too weighty for us to lift. We had both glimpsed how the other would be, and we could never un-see it.

Now I see you once a year, when you open up the cottage for those few precious weeks in August. And you bring me my summer boy. Because all along you had your own Rory, already formed, already growing, already more than a blue line. That last unplanned baby.

And when we meet on the beach path, and you say hello, I catch Rory's ghost in your eyes. And your wife looks puzzled, and automatically reaches for my summer boy's hand.

Immortal

by Krishan Coupland

Dizzy with sim-wine, and in the dim light of the bedroom, I didn't notice her scars. We fell into bed together and peeled away clothes to the sounds of distant fireworks. She was beautiful, I thought, slim and etched with gold where the streetlights slipped in through the blind. She held me tightly and whispered things I couldn't hear.

It was only the next morning when I woke to find her sleeping that I saw the marks on her back. A dark central scar surrounded by rings of silver buried just beneath the surface of the skin. I recognised them at once, even though I'd never seen them on a real person before. My hand hovered, wanting to feel the beat of her mechanical heart, the stretch and flex of her synthetic lungs.

"You didn't tell me you'd had the implants," I said, when she finally woke. I'd dressed while she slept. The sight of the scars had left me feeling small and fleshy.

She stretched, unconcerned. "Yeah. A while ago now." Even having just woken from sleep her hair was perfect. I marvelled at the fact that she had ever even taken an interest in me.

"How old are you?" I said.

"Twenty-five."

"I mean, how old really?"

She shrugged. "I'm twenty-five forever."

Sober now I could see it in her eyes: the little streaks of silver that would never fade, that would keep her strong and healthy long after I was ash.

Son of God – the pin-up

by Sharon Boyle

My church prayed before a dreamboat Jesus. Twice on Sundays we tilted our faces to Him and although His hands were nailed, His ribs gashed and His feet squished awkwardly together, it was plain to all, He did that crucifix proud. Those wooden Californian waves were bouffant and the muscle to skin ratio faultless. If He had chosen to shake that salon-perfect hair and hop down with,

"Patti, hun, let's you and me get outta here",

I'd have pow-wowed out a "Hell, yeh."

But then I moved north to stay with cousin Velma. She lived in an armpit of a town made freezing by the sun's reluctance to go anywhere near the place.

"Your Jesus has mange," I whispered first time in her church, sitting all sweatered-up in one of her cast-offs.

"He's not meant to be in tippity-top condition, Patti. He suffered. For us. Jesus was an awesome man."

Velma thought me a screw-up – the fact I hung out with bikers and glued myself to mirrors, fretting over looks, especially my non-salon, non-bouffant hair.

"You're going to hell, Patti," she liked to say. "Just the same as Lucifer, except that unlike Lucifer you've never even been angelic."

We spoke less and less to one another, partly 'cos she was a high-nosed holy holy and partly 'cos we agreed on nothing. One Sunday she stopped speaking to me entirely. Apparently, someone had gussied up Jesus with a biker jacket and bandana and felt-tipped a couple of hearts on His sacred cheek. Velma did not snitch for fear it would reflect on her like a tainted mirror, which it would of course; hell, yeh. But as she climbed the ladder to scrub the demon muck off her Saviour, she probably cussed the very life out of me. Jesus was again a regular prayer-worthy fellow, but now that he had been a Hell's Angel and still wore a faded heart on His cheek like a defiant tattoo, he was indeed awesome. On that, Velma and I did agree. And even though Velma broke her Carmelite silence to hiss that Heaven would kick my fat ass straight outta their gates if I dared try enter, I would bow my head in pantomime guilt and think at least I'd be a hell of a lot warmer than in Armpit Town.

Hidden treasure

by Tric Kearney

A perfect rainbow on the gable wall catches my eye. Its painter, a single ray of sunlight, emerges from a chink in the seventy years of dirt coating the attic window. Bursting through, it strikes an object hidden within an old tin box, fragmenting its light into a kaleidoscope of colours, before splashing them onto the bare brick wall for admiration.

Tip toeing through the litter of bygone days, I follow the sunbeam's finger pointing where I must go. What magical object has caught its light? Hidden from view, scattered among various odds and ends, is a miniature, finely cut, glass perfume bottle.

"Junk" my mother would have said of all within the box, without investigation.

I hold it as if it were made of the most precious glass. This was my mother's perfume bottle, faithfully filled with her favourite scent. The full stop in her preparations for a special occasion.

Removing the tear-drop lid, I listen for the quiet pop of the seal breaking. Raising the delicate bottle to just beneath my nose, I close my eyes, as the faintest scent of childhood fills my soul. Memories I'd forgotten, envelope me. With each breath, childhood and adolescence agonies and ecstasies rush by, until but one moment remains; my mother, beckoning me to her dressing table where she dots a spot of perfume behind her ears and mine.

As her image fades, I place my finger over the small opening and tip the bottle, hoping for more. It's empty. Perhaps it has spilled or evaporated in the lifetime since Mother last used it? I breathe in once more, wishing to fill a void I'd not known existed up to moments ago.

Replacing the bottle amongst the other gems I turn it left and right hoping to recreate the rainbow, but the sun has lost interest. I pick my way back across the junk ridden room before pausing to look at the gable wall. The rainbow is gone, the sun no longer pointing.

But as I close the door, the faint scent of childhood follows me.

Things that used to be safe

by Natalia Theodoridou

1. Looking at the sky
2. Rain
3. Rain falling on your face
4. Washing your hands
5. Brushing your teeth
6. Washing the dishes
7. Drinking water
8. Walking through damp fields in bloom on a Saturday afternoon
9. Queuing in open spaces, looking at the sky
10. Saying your name, waiting your turn
11. Saying your name in implied protest
12. Saying a lover's name
13. Thinking of birds in flight
14. Thinking of having children
15. Looking at the sky, speculating whether it's about to rain
16. Having children
17. Bathing your child
18. Thinking of a lake
19. Standing at the edge of cliffs
20. Standing at the edge of cliffs, looking down
21. Giving your children maritime names (like Marina, Bertha, or Finn)
22. Remembering waterfalls
23. Remembering the weightlessness of bodies in water
24. Getting nostalgic of days and joys long gone
25. Taking a shower
26. Taking a bath
27. Walking fully clothed into a lake
28. Doing laundry
29. Momentarily forgetting the acid-bite apocalypse of rain
30. Saying "I am thirsty"
31. Saying "I miss walking in the rain '
32. Making tea
33. Making coffee
34. Looking at the sky

The mountain cherry tree corps

by Amanda Huggins

Marnie: just turned seventeen, life unwinding before her like a bright silken thread. As she walked through the door of the Imperial War Museum she reached for her boyfriend's hand. For a few minutes they moved silently around the vast space, glancing at the uniforms in glass cases, looking up at the fragile planes. The bombs unnerved her; even in their benign state their shape instinctively aroused fear.

She stopped at some photographs. Chilling images of a mushroom cloud; a bleak, broken wasteland; glass bottles melted into deformed shapes. Then she saw the plane. A single cherry blossom painted on its side. The young face of a pilot: Akito Watashi. In his funeral portrait, he stared straight ahead. He had kind eyes.

Marnie squeezed her boyfriend's hand, but she didn't stop reading. The Yamazakura-tai - the Mountain Cherry Blossom Corps. Falling blossoms signifying death in battle. Eyes wide open in the face of the enemy. The battle cry: You and I are cherry blossoms in season... Every flower knows it must die. We will die gloriously, then, for our homeland.

She noticed a Japanese woman patiently waiting until they moved away. They smiled at each other, and the woman bowed slightly as they swapped places in front of the display. As they walked away, Marnie saw her reach out towards the photograph of Akito Watashi and gently touch the glass with her finger.

When they stepped back out into the sunlight she walked quietly at Pete's side towards the trees. She understood that she must tell him now. It was there between them; tiny, unacknowledged, barely formed.

"Pete?"

"Yes?"

She could see the future in his kind eyes, and knew that if she asked he would do the good, right thing. Marnie thought of the pilot with the kind eyes, about to sacrifice his life, and knew that she couldn't ask Pete to do the same.

"The museum was sad" she said instead, and he kissed her hand.

As they walked away, she saw the Japanese woman again. Their eyes met before the woman disappeared into the weekend crowds. Marnie watched her walk away beneath the bare-branched cherry trees.

It was then that she saw the leaf; a single speck of pale green hope, taking a chance ahead of the blossom.

Without hesitation she turned to Pete and started again.

"Pete, there's something I must tell you."

Orange

by Mark Dixon

At the centre of it all lay a memory that turned out to be not true at all. The memory in question was mine, at least I thought it had been mine, but, in the end, it turned out to be something else. Perhaps, I had taken ownership of its cotton finery when I was drunk. Yes, that must have been the case. It must have lodged at some opportune moment, and from there it's troubling repercussions issued.

It was a simple recollection, too straightforward to be of concern just yet - a jazz note, you might say, bent upwards in a promise of musical flourish that never materialised.

I was hit by the import of the fabrication when driving home from a dreary Sunday's dinner with my parents. I needed petrol, and, after refuelling, sat in the car weighing up all that had transpired. The service station bathed in the demeaning light of street lamps, all colour reduced to the shade of a crackling bonfire, an orange monoculture that sat empty save for the comings and goings of a fast food restaurant at the far side of the carpark.

"Don't be ridiculous," I remembered my father saying. That was all. Of course, dinner continued without a scene, but later, when I replayed the events of the afternoon, I realised how right my father had been. Right, because the memory in question could never have happened in the way that I recalled. The facts - the simple objective truth of the situation didn't add up.

Here, watching the comings and goings, the peripheries began to collapse too. If, I pondered, if that simple memory was so palpably untrue then what else might be up for grabs? For the memory in question was a layer of tissue on which other memories were laid. Each snatch or smell and utterance forming a helix of meaning that brought me quivering into the present. If one link, especially one a simple as this, were untrue then it stood to reason that others might be questionable.

Under the orange glare I began to rake through the rolodex of my life - formative memories filed first, the latter pushed into whatever crevice would hold them. This was the palimpsest of me, and even then, while processing and filing, I realised that some moments were so oddly placed that I fancied that they had never existed either.

I turned on the car for a little warmth and saw that a hatchback with trims and spoilers had pulled up in front of where I was parked. Inside, sat teenagers peeling burgers from wrappers. The car full of life, with hats worn the wrong way, a girl squeezed sideways between two youths in the back. I couldn't help but stare, and, when caught doing so, one of the men shouted something in my direction. Of course, I made for the motorway, the young man staring at me as I left, a finger drawn across his throat as I sped into the darkness.

Cutting the cord

by Amanda O'Callaghan

He buys champagne on the way home from work. His first child - the secret one - has come of age.

He stands in the kitchen with his wife, staring past her into the garden. He winces at the thought of what those eighteen years have cost him. That pointless conference, the ridiculous plush of the hotel, the sales guys jumping naked into the pool. No one where they ought to be.

He pictures himself in the garden's far corner, reading the letter that came for him. The sprawl of her writing. That world without email, without phones small enough for hidden things. How he pinched the edge of the paper as if it were on fire. *Pregnant. Baby.* In the thresh of words, that was all he saw.

The light's fading now. Above the street's elegant gables, stars appear. He chinks two glasses onto the marble bench. Thinks of the lies that came after that letter.

"You're off your game, son. Anything wrong?" his father had said, early on, as they walked towards the last hole.

"What could be wrong?" he'd replied, slicing the ball.

But migraines pulsed in his head. Sleep deserted him. When he blew the promotion two years in, he fell apart. Trapped and panicking, he told his wife everything. A time like this, night coming.

There were no raised voices. They stayed together, moving through these rooms. But he can't forget the way her fury seeped into the bones of the house, hung, waiting, in sunless corners. Even now, the clink of cutlery in a still room brings him almost to his knees.

Years later, when a card was left for him at work, scratched in a teenage hand, he brought it to her like an offering. He watched, gulping the air in small, grateful sobs, as she singed it on the gas cooktop until it was a tight curl of black ash.

He pours, stealing a glance at his wife. She's looking light-headed already, he thinks. She's totting figures in her head.

"Thank God that's over," he says.

"About time," she answers.

They sip in silence. Rich, smooth. A clean finish. She touches his arm, mentions the cruise again.

"We could leave the kids behind," she whispers, nodding at the boys in the next room. "It would be so nice to get away."

He doesn't answer. Lets her words circle in his mind. In the garden, the automatic light flashes on. They both look out, as if something unexpected might be there.

Stars everywhere now, reaching towards the coast. A promising night, he thinks. He drains his glass, gives his wife a smile he knows she'll like. She drinks contentedly, taking the measure of the room with a triumphant tilt of her chin.

He looks outside, beyond the garden and the neat enclave of houses. He doesn't think of a cruise. He thinks of moonlight on a stretching road. A new car. Loud, the engine roaring. Something faster. Something much, much smaller.

ACKNOWLEDGEMENTS

All of the flash fiction pieces were published by InkTears in their
monthly newsletter, between 2012 and 2019.

Several of these pieces were published previously in literary
magazines or anthologies. We thank the authors and publishers for
letting us reprint these stories here in this collected format.

www.ingramcontent.com/pod-product-compliance
Lightning Source LLC
Chambersburg PA
CBHW020402130626
46549CB00006B/2394